Heather Gemmen Wilson

wesleyan
publishing
house

Indianapolis, Indiana

Copyright © 2008 by Wesleyan Publishing House
Published by Wesleyan Publishing House
Indianapolis, Indiana 46250
Printed in the United States of America
ISBN: 978-0-89827-352-6

Library of Congress Cataloging-in-Publication Data

Wilson, Heather Gemmen.
  Lydia Barnes and the escape from Shark Bay / Heather Gemmen Wilson.
     p. cm.
  Summary: Lydia, her father, and Ben make both friends and enemies
while in Jamaica to check on a school established by Global Relief and
Outreach, when an evil woman goes to great lengths to protect the
reputation of her resort.
  ISBN 978-0-89827-352-6
  [1. Resorts--Fiction. 2. Missionaries--Fiction. 3. Kidnapping--Fiction.
4. Arson--Fiction. 5. Christian life--Fiction. 6. Jamaica--Fiction. 7.
Mystery and detective stories--Fiction.] I. Title.
  PZ7.W6952Lyf 2008
  [Fic]--dc22
                                        2007049188

All Scripture quotations, unless otherwise indicated, are taken from the HOLY
BIBLE, NEW INTERNATIONAL VERSION ®. NIV ®. Copyright 1973, 1978, 1984 by
the International Bible Society. Used by permission of Zondervan. All rights
reserved.

Scripture quotations marked (KJV) are taken from THE HOLY BIBLE, KING JAMES
VERSION.

All rights reserved. No part of this publication may be reproduced, stored in a
retrieval system, or transmitted in any form or by any means—electronic,
mechanical, photocopy, recording or any other—except for brief quotations in
printed reviews, without the prior written permission of the publisher.

Contents

For Mary

A Note to You

hen I was a girl living in the wide-open spaces of Oklahoma, I loved mystery stories. Sometimes, as I followed the adventures of my hero, Nancy Drew, the story was so intense that I could barely turn the pages to see what would happen next. Little did I know that I would someday experience many similar adventures of my own.

When I became a follower of Jesus, he opened the world to me. I began to see that it was not just storybook heroes who could have adventures—regular kids like I was could go out and do amazing things to make the world a better place. Remember, when you and I pray the Lord's Prayer saying "Thy will be done on earth as it is in heaven," God wants *us* to make that happen!

Now I'm pleased to introduce you to a wonderful new hero named Lydia Barnes. I know you'll be thrilled to follow her adventures in faraway places like Africa, Jamaica, and Jerusalem. As you do, remember this amazing truth—*Kids can change the world!*

I hope this book will be the beginning of your own adventure. I am looking forward to hearing about the awesome, creative things *you* will do to make a difference in your community and in the world.

Jo Anne Lyon
Executive Director
World Hope International

1

Emerald Puke

The small plane rattled like a dying refrigerator.

Lydia Barnes forced herself to open her eyes. If she was going to die, she wanted to be able to see it happen.

The inside of the plane reminded her of the inside of a minivan—except for all the knobs and controls up front. Her dad was sitting beside the pilot in a bucket seat. He turned around, grinning at her like he had just handed her tickets to a Hawk Nelson concert. As if this were fun. "Isn't this great?" he yelled.

Lydia turned to look out the side window. Below her the Caribbean Sea shone emerald in the sunlight. They were flying so low that she could see dolphins bounding along in the ocean below them. At least if the plane crashed it wouldn't have far to go. Lydia unclenched her fingers from the leather seat. A little bit.

They were flying from the east side of the island of Jamaica to the west side along the southern shore. The sky in front of them was a stunning mix of blue and pink as the sun was getting ready to set; behind them was a mass of white, puffy clouds.

Lydia could hardly believe it was the middle of January. Her friends back home in Indianapolis would be huddling up in warm coats looking at gray skies from a dreary schoolyard. She was most definitely having a better Monday than they were. Even though she was in a rattling fridge five hundred feet up in the sky.

"You want to fly?" the pilot yelled to Lydia's dad over the moaning of the motor. The pilot was a white American who looked like a skateboarder, with long blond hair and cargo shorts. Lydia wondered if he was even old enough to have his driver's license.

Of course, people never thought her dad, Frank Barnes, was as old as he was either—and he had the same it's-all-good attitude. Frank wore dark green convertible pants, just like hers, and a black Nike Dri-Fit T-shirt. Behind his aviator glasses, Lydia could see the look on her dad's face at the pilot's offer. He was as excited as a kid who had been offered an endless supply of cotton candy, but he tried to play it cool.

"Sure!" he yelled back. He grabbed the wheel in front of him—well, it was more like a horseshoe than a wheel—and looked at the pilot for further instruction.

"Nothing to it!" the pilot yelled, letting go of his own wheel. "Just hold 'er steady."

Frank held her steady for about a minute, and then he looked at the pilot again. "You care if I play a bit?"

The pilot laughed. "Go ahead."

And Frank, without any concern for his terrified-of-flying daughter in the backseat, zipped up and down, side to side along the coast. The dolphins disappeared, and the green water suddenly looked to Lydia more like puke than emeralds.

"You want a turn?" the pilot yelled to Lydia after five minutes or so.

"Yeah!" Frank yelled. "Great idea!" Before Lydia could say anything, he unbuckled and squeezed between the bucket seats to join Lydia in the back. "Go on," Frank said, grinning.

"I can't fly!" Lydia squealed.

"Well, you'd better, because no one else is." The pilot lifted his hands and put them behind his head.

Lydia jumped up—and the seat belt she had forgotten to unbuckle yanked her back down.

"Hurry," the pilot said, closing his eyes. "This thing doesn't fly itself, you know."

Lydia scrambled to the cockpit. The pilot appeared to be snoring, though she wasn't so dumb that she didn't know he was faking. Still, he wasn't flying. And her dad was in the backseat. She gripped the horseshoe in her suddenly sweating palms—and the plane plummeted.

"Aaaaahhhhh!" Lydia screamed, and yanked the wheel so that they shot almost straight back up again.

"You're wilder than your dad!" the pilot yelled, wide awake now with his hands ready to take the wheel again. He was grinning, though. "Come on. Straighten 'er out. Gently. This baby responds to the slightest touch."

Lydia, more gently this time, pushed the wheel forward and the plane slowly eased down. When they were level, she held the wheel perfectly still.

"Great job!" the pilot yelled, placing his hands back behind his head. "You'll be able to land it without a problem."

"What?" Lydia screamed. When both the men laughed, she groaned. She couldn't believe she had fallen for that. "I could easily land it," she shot at them.

They hooted with laughter, and Lydia relaxed. It really was quite amazing to be flying, and she was glad they'd made her try it.

A few minutes later static came from the pilot's radio and a man's voice spoke out. He had a Jamaican accent. "Bill, mon. Are you on de schedule?"

Lydia loved accents, but the Jamaican accent was her most favorite of all. It sounded like someone reciting poetry because all the sentences seemed to have a rhythm to them.

The pilot picked up the walkie-talkie and spoke into it. "Yeah, Mo, right on time. You got another passenger for me?"

"I don' think you should come back tonight, Bill. We got de edge of a storm comin'."

Bill took over the wheel again and veered left so they could look out their side windows in the direction they had just come from. Lydia saw that the fluffy white cotton candy had been transformed into dark gray fists. "Wow! Yeah, I can see it," Bill said. "I thought this one was heading back out to sea."

"You cannot control de weather, mon. De weather, it is in God's hands."

Bill pulled the plane on course again, his face grim.

Lydia stuck her head toward the back and said to her dad, "Jamaica's not supposed to have hurricanes in January!" She had seen TV news stories about hurricane victims, and before they left for this trip, Lydia had made her dad promise that they wouldn't get caught in a storm like that. "Well, I can't promise," he'd said, "but I can tell you that about 97 percent of hurricane activity is from June 1 to November 30, and if anything happens off season, it's likely to be December or May. So don't worry." And yet there was the storm, creeping up behind them.

"Relax. It's not a hurricane," her dad said. "Besides, I can't control de weather, mon."

It was a bad time for a joke. Which was typical of her dad.

Lydia spent the rest of the flight looking out the side window—craning her neck to try to see behind them. The clouds seemed to be moving faster than her best friend Amy toward her latest crush. Lydia didn't have to stress for long, though, because five minutes later the pilot landed the little Cessna smoothly.

Then Lydia had new things to stress about.

Three Jamaican men came out of the little shack beside the single runway and began unloading luggage before Frank was even out of the plane. "That's okay," Frank called to them as he scrambled from the backseat. "I'll get that."

"It's alright, mon," said one of the men, smiling so huge all his teeth were showing. His dreadlocks bounced as he talked. "We help you, mon."

Frank smiled back and took the two packs from them. "Thanks again, but we don't have much. I think we can handle it."

"No problem, mon!" the guy held up his hands like Frank had pointed a gun at him, even though Lydia thought her dad had sounded perfectly friendly. "I don' mean no harm, mon!"

Frank laughed and went to shake hands with the pilot, who was locking up the plane. Lydia was impressed by her dad's easy manner. She would have apologized and assured the Jamaican guy that she hadn't been trying to be mean; but when the guy laughed himself and followed her dad, telling him he had some cold Red Stripe for him, which was the favorite local drink, she realized his look of being hurt was just an act.

"Thanks, Bill," Frank said, ignoring the Jamaicans who were still trying to sell them stuff. "It was a great flight."

"Sure beats the shuttle, doesn't it?" Bill said. They could have taken a bus across the island and not arrived here for another four or five hours—which meant they would have been on the road in a rickety tin can during the storm. Lydia could hardly believe they had finally done something right. Maybe this trip would be calm and uneventful for once. She was ready for a break from all her adventures.

Lydia's dad had taken the job as senior consultant for Global Relief and Outreach (GRO), which meant he, with Lydia, had to jet all over the world developing and supporting mission posts. Her first adventure in Liberia, Africa, a couple of months ago, had brought her face-to-face with a rebel warlord—not to mention a tricky private teacher her dad had hired—before finding the mother lode of buried treasure. From there Lydia and her dad went to spend the Christmas holidays in the Holy Land—where Lydia thought she'd either be blown up by terrorists or thrown in jail for theft and vandalism. Long story.

After their trip to the Middle East, Lydia and her dad had spent two blessed weeks at home with absolutely no adventures. Lydia home schooled herself, while her dad looked for a new tutor—since the one Frank had hired for Lydia had stayed in Africa with the VanderHooks to help out in the medical clinic and to tutor Lydia's friend Ben. Poor Ben. Lydia was using the same course material Ben was using for now. But she and her dad were meeting up with the new tutor here in Jamaica, and Lydia hoped this woman would get a curriculum that wasn't so boring. She also hoped the new teacher wouldn't be as bizarre and mysterious as Mrs. Hinkle had been. Hink was nothing but trouble.

No matter what, Lydia figured it was a good time for a break on a Caribbean island.

Lydia walked with her dad and the pilot toward the parking lot, where a bunch of taxis waited, and all the men followed.

"Where you goin'? I take you!" they called out.

"I braid for you," a woman said, running her fingers through Lydia's long, dark hair. "Very pretty!"

"I got de good stuff for you, mon," another whispered near Frank's ear, and Lydia knew he was talking about drugs. Her dad had told her that many Americans bought drugs here while on vacation, and they often ended up in Jamaica's poorly run prisons.

"Which resort are you going to?" Bill asked. "I might tag along."

"We're actually going inland to meet some friends," Frank said. "They're picking us up here sometime this afternoon."

Lydia inwardly groaned. They'd been traveling all day, and she absolutely didn't feel like sitting around any longer. Of course, she should be used to it by now. She was a world traveler, after all—which meant she knew what it was like to sit for about ten thousand hours squished in a little seat on a plane or on hard chairs in some airport, feeling greasy and grumpy all the while.

"I suggest that you don't wait around here," Bill said, reaching out for the door handle of a cab. "If your friends don't show, you'll be stuck here in the middle of nowhere during a massive storm. You'd be better off waiting in a hotel lobby."

Frank looked up at the clouds, which were growing darker by the minute.

"Come on," Bill said.

Frank and Lydia climbed into the cab and Bill asked the driver about hotels. "You got no reservation, mon?" the driver asked, shaking his head. "Den I take you to de Bayside Hotel. Dey help you. No problem." The driver pulled onto the two-lane highway on the wrong side of the road—"*Other* side," her dad would have said if Lydia had said that out loud—and began beeping at each passing car.

Bill didn't look as if he thought everything was okay. As for Frank, he was holding his cell phone to his ear looking a bit worried himself. He smiled suddenly and said, "Oh, good! I was afraid I wouldn't reach you." While Frank talked, Lydia stared at the shed-sized houses they passed that seemed even smaller and less inviting than the homes she had seen in Africa. After a few minutes of conversation, Frank hung up and said to the driver, "Could you take us to the Luxury Resort after you drop Bill off? Our plans have changed."

"De Luxury Resort, sah?" the driver said. "Ah you sure? I think you like de hotel better."

Frank looked up quickly. "Is there something wrong with the Luxury Resort?"

"No, sah, nutting wrong," the driver said, flashing a smile in the mirror. "No problem."

Frank shrugged and turned to Lydia. "Turns out your tutor arrived this morning and decided to wait for us out at the Luxury Resort. I had her rent a car, and we can take that down to the mission."

"Tonight?"

Frank looked out the window and saw the black clouds overhead. "We'll see," he said.

By the time they dropped Bill off, raindrops the size of quarters were splattering against the car windows. Bill waved goodbye and disappeared into a glamorous resort. Once they started moving again, Lydia couldn't see through the heavy rain to the other side of the road. She wondered how the driver was staying on the road. But after a few minutes, he pulled off the highway, waited at a huge iron gate for a moment until it slowly opened, and followed the drive right into the marble building, where a bellboy quickly jumped to their service.

The Luxury Resort lived up to its name. The floors, walls, and ceilings were all made of marble. All outer doorways had no actual doors, so the freshness of the outdoors could be felt inside. Even with the heavy rain, not a drop entered this magnificent entryway. There must have been awnings even beyond the walls that Lydia could not see. One bellboy took their luggage; another offered Frank a glass of wine, which he declined; and another gestured toward silky couches.

Lydia hardly noticed any of that, though. What she was staring at was better than all the luxury in the world. Jumping out of a hammock and running toward her was the one person in the world she most wanted to see.

2
Foxy Lynx

Ben VanderHook looked as though he were about to hug Lydia, but he suddenly stopped short and stuck out his hand. Lydia, feeling a bit embarrassed herself for screaming at the sight of him, shook his hand and excitedly whispered—so that all the people watching would quit gaping—"What are you doing here?"

"Visiting you," Ben said with a huge smile. When Lydia first met Ben only two months ago, she had thought he was the biggest geek in the world. Short with messy black hair, he always had a zit poking out somewhere. Ben was Korean by birth, but he lived in Africa with his adoptive white parents and talked like any old American boy, but with a squeaky voice. She'd thought there was nothing special about him until she got to know him—which was right away. Soon after they'd met, Lydia and Ben were plunged into a dangerous quest to find hidden treasure and needed to depend on each other for their very lives.

Now Lydia considered Ben her very best friend in all the world, but in a different way than Amy, her best friend from back home. Amy was fun to laugh with and to share silly secrets with, but Ben understood a part of her life that no one else could. He was with her when she was discovering the bigger world and her own faith, and he still didn't think she was crazy.

"Visiting me?" She laughed and turned to her dad. "Why didn't you tell me?"

Frank laughed too. "It was a surprise."

"I suppose," a gruff voice from behind Lydia said, "that I also am a surprise?"

Lydia turned around and saw a short, skinny lady with her hair up in a bun wearing a lavender and black polka-dotted bikini under a silver mesh cover-up. "Hink!" Lydia exclaimed.

"Mrs. Hinkle, if you please," said the old woman with her lips pulled down and her eyelids nearly closed.

"Your new tutor," Frank said, winking.

"But—"

"I'll admit I had to do a little begging," Frank said.

"But—"

"Turns out," Hink said, her nose still held high, "that I am much more qualified to be your teacher than to poke people with needles."

Lydia wasn't so sure about that. Hink seemed to be a master at getting under people's skin. And maybe it was worse than that. In Africa, Ben and Lydia were certain the person who was trying to sabotage their efforts to find the hidden treasure was none other than Mrs. Hinkle. In the end, the teacher turned out to be all sugar and spice, but Lydia still had her doubts.

"And my dad said I could go with her to meet you here," Ben said in a hurry. "I'll go back to the States with you next week and meet up with Mom and Dad there. They're on sabbatical."

"Which means they're taking a little break from their work right now," Frank explained. "And they're also going to be look-ing for a nurse to replace Hink—er—Mrs. Hinkle."

Before the reunion could go on much longer, a twenty-something Jamaican woman wearing a well-fitted navy suit with an orange scarf approached them. She had very dark skin, contrasted sharply by the whites of her almond-shaped eyes. Her shiny hair was pulled tight against her head. Her thin face, plump lips, and jutting cheekbones gave her the look of an exotic model, but her smile did not appear posed. "Excuse me, sah," she said to Frank. "My name is Ms. Young. I am de assistant manager here." She shook his hand and then gestured for him to take a seat on the silky couches they were standing next to. "It would be my pleasure to you."

Frank looked at Hink. "Did you check in?"

Hink shook her head. "I wasn't entirely certain of your plans, so the hotel kindly let us enjoy the facilities until you arrived. Are we staying?" She nodded toward the young lady as if Frank were being rude by ignoring her.

Frank remained standing, and the young woman stepped back. "Sah, you are welcome to take more time—"

"Forgive me, my dear," interrupted an American voice as silky as the plush couches. Lydia looked over to see an elegant woman approaching them. Beautiful, with perfectly straight, jet-black hair, the lady wore a black suit that moved as if it were a part of her trim body and smiled as though she were handing out free iPods to everyone. "You wouldn't think of going back out into that terrible storm, would you?" She placed a hand on Lydia's shoulder protectively.

"I'm afraid we don't have much of a choice," Frank said, sighing heavily and picking up the pack he had set down.

"Of course you have a choice," the purred. "You always have a choice." She smiled again, and Frank smiled back. "Let me introduce myself. I am Helena Lynx, the owner of this resort." She reached over to shake Frank's hand, and she let it linger there as she sat down. Frank, whose hand was still in hers, was forced to sit down beside her. He didn't seem to mind much. Hink sat down across from them, leaning forward as if she wanted to be included in the conversation.

Lydia looked at Ben and shrugged her shoulders. This could be interesting.

"It would be my pleasure to set you up in little suite perfect for the four of you." Mrs. Lynx looked at each of the four people she was referring to, captivating them with her smile. "I would feel positively wicked"—she paused, seeming to enjoy the word—"if I were to send you out into that weather."

And just like that, Lydia found herself registered in an all-inclusive Caribbean resort for *two* nights—Mrs. Lynx was so sorry, but she did not have any packages available for one night only. Here, all Lydia's needs and desires were to be met, on the guarantee of the owner herself.

Lydia wanted to go exploring with Ben, but it was dark and storming; so after a quick dinner at one of the indoor restaurants in the resort, they all went to the suite to watch a movie and then hit the sack. Lydia didn't care that she had to share a room with Hink and hardly noticed that a storm was rattling the windows. She fell asleep before her head hit the pillow, and she woke up to sunshine streaming into the lovely olive green room.

Hink was already showered and dressed and on her way out the door for a walk on the beach. Lydia stood for a half hour in the shower, using up all the thick shampoo and conditioner while the music of Corinne Bailey Rae wafted through the bathroom speakers. When she finally convinced herself to get out of the shower, Lydia pulled a couple oversized, fluffy, pale yellow towels from the heating rack, and wrapped one around her body and one around her hair. Then she sat on the bed to paint her toenails. "This is the life," she said out loud. Being a missionary certainly had its perks.

When she was finally dressed in a cute cotton sundress, with her favorite swimsuit underneath, and bright red sandals, Lydia admired herself in the mirror, sucking in her belly. Mrs. Lynx would certainly approve. She knocked on the door to her dad's room and opened it a crack. The room was dark, and the guys were still snoring. "Wake up, Daddy!" she said, opening the curtains. "You're wasting your day!"

"I thought I was using it very wisely," he said sleepily, but he sat up and stretched. "Come on, Ben," he said to the figure in the other bed, who had pulled the blankets over his head. "Let's go sleep on the beach."

Lydia went back to her room to blow-dry her damp hair. The guys banged on her door before she even finished getting ready.

"Where's Hink?" Frank asked.

"She's out walking. Can we eat breakfast now? I'm starved!"

After a short walk through the palm-studded path leading from the two-storied cottage-styled buildings that housed the resort guests, they found Hink sitting on a deck outside the main lobby, watching the waves roll gently onto the beach. People were sunbathing, sailing, walking, playing volleyball, swimming in the pools and ocean, or snorkeling. The only signs of the storm were some bent and broken branches on a few of the palm trees. Otherwise all the storm debris had already been whisked away.

"It's not half-bad," Hink said, gesturing toward the large buffet breakfast being served. "And there's plenty of it."

Ben, Lydia, and Frank piled their plates full of crisp bacon, juicy sausage, foaming scrambled eggs, thick waffles with strawberries and rich whipped cream—all covered in gooey maple syrup. And that was just the start. When they polished off their first serving, they went back for a cooked-to-order omelet with some golden fried potatoes and a freshly whipped fruit smoothie.

"Ugh!" Lydia moaned, pushing her plate away after she had eaten everything. "Why did you let me do that? I've never eaten so much in my life!"

"Tea or coffee, miss?" a waiter asked at that moment.

Lydia smiled. "Tea would be wonderful, thank you."

After the tea was poured and the basket of pastries refilled, the waiter moved on. Lydia selected a scrumptious-looking éclair and looked up to see all three of the others staring at her. "What?" she asked.

"I thought you were stuffed," Ben said.

Lydia dropped her éclair like it was a hot coal. "Oh, yeah!" she said. "Ohhhh! I'm so mad at myself. I was trying to lose weight!"

"Lose weight?" Frank asked, picking up the éclair she had dropped and stuffing a huge portion into his mouth. "Why?"

"I'm getting fat!" Lydia said. "You shouldn't have let me eat all that."

"You're not fat," Frank said with his mouth full. "But even if you were, it wouldn't be my fault. You make your own choices."

"You're absolutely *not* fat," Hink said emphatically, even angrily. "Girls these days!" Hink herself was as thin as the stray kitten Lydia had once saved, but that was clearly not the point. "However," Hink said, turning toward Lydia's dad, "it would be your fault, Frank, if she were. She's only a child and your responsibility."

"'Even a child is known by her actions,'" Frank said, quoting some Bible verse, which was typical of him. "I can't be with her every moment telling her what to eat when. She has to be responsible for herself. If I dictated everything to her, she wouldn't know how to make good decisions for herself. If she's fat—"

"I'm not fat!" Lydia said.

"No, of course you're not," Frank said, laughing. "That's because you choose to gorge yourself to the point of bursting only for special occasions like today."

"Let's go swimming," Ben said.

"I can't swim!" Lydia said. "I'd sink to the bottom like a rock."

"Because you're fat?" Ben teased.

"Aarrggghh!" Lydia yelled. "You people drive me crazy." But they didn't, really. She even had a kind thought about Mrs. Hinkle when the old woman, a moment later, announced that she was going to join the scuba diving class that started in a few minutes. Lydia had to admire Hink for doing so many interesting things even though she was ancient.

"Cool!" Frank said. "You kids should do that too. Since I got suckered into spending a couple days here, we may as well take advantage of it." He already had his scuba license and said he'd rather do some sailing instead. Lydia was thrilled. She and Ben jumped up to start their day of fun. Guests of the resort ("More like stockholders at this price," Frank had grumbled) were free to do any of the many activities that were offered and to eat free at any restaurant any time of the day or night.

The scuba class met in a little swimming pool at the far end of the resort where the students had to listen to a long lecture about safety. Then they took turns trying to breathe under water—sounding like Darth Vader the whole time—which was as difficult as keeping your eye open when someone was poking it. Ben mastered the trick before Lydia, but she beat him in the swimming test in the ocean a little while later.

"Now what?" Ben asked when the two-hour class was over. They weren't allowed to scuba dive until they finished the next day's class, and they were still stuffed from breakfast. Hink was off to the racquetball courts, and Lydia could see the bright yellow sail of her dad's boat zipping around just past the snorkelers.

"Let's walk down the beach," Lydia said. "Once we get sweating hot, we'll swim."

It was about noon, and many people were already in the water, so Ben and Lydia had to weave in and out of groups of people. They walked more than a half hour, past one resort after another, until they left all the tourists behind. The sand became rocky and the rocks became solid—and they came to a cliff wall that went far into the water.

"Let's climb up and see what's on the other side," Lydia said. It would take some work to get past the bottom part that was rocky and steep, but Lydia could see a gentle slope with green grass just ten feet up.

"No way," Ben said. "I'm hot and tired. We were gonna go swimming, remember?"

"Okay, then let's swim around the rocks." Lydia was just sure that whatever was on the other side of that cliff held some sort of mystery.

Ben looked around. "There are no lifeguards or people around here, Lyd. I don't think we should. Let's just go back."

Lydia gave the cliff one long look, and then turned around. Ben was probably right. She didn't need to know what was on the other side of that cliff. Plus, she reminded herself, she didn't want an adventure on this trip.

As they walked away, though, Lydia couldn't resist another glance. And for just a second she thought she saw something flash on top of the hill.

"Ben! Someone's up there!"

Ben turned around and they both stood perfectly still in the silence.

"Uh-uh," Ben finally said. "No one's there. Come on."

But Lydia knew he didn't believe his own words, because she had to almost run to keep up with him.

3
Hidden Danger

The walk back to the resort seemed much longer. And by now Lydia and Ben were hungry and hot. As soon as they got to a touristy part of the beach where a lifeguard watched, they dove in the water to cool off. Then they set off again for the Luxury Resort so they could eat.

By 1:30, Ben was stuffing his face with a greasy chimichanga and fried rice, and Lydia was picking at what was supposed to be a fresh salad. Clearly this resort did better at providing fattening food than healthy choices. Or maybe Lydia was just spoiled by the incredible fresh salads she'd eaten every day in Israel a few weeks earlier.

"You're missing out, Lyd," Ben said.

They were sitting on stools at the counter of a small thatch-roofed restaurant right on the beach with the sun on their backs. Hink and Frank were both lounging on lawn chairs behind them.

Lydia purposely kept her eyes cast away from Ben's greasy food. "I have enough self-control to stay away from *that*," she told him.

Before Ben could remind her of the morning's gorging, Mrs. Lynx's voiced eased into the conversation. "Not that it's any of my business," she said with a smile as she sidled up beside Lydia, "but why would you even want to try to resist food this scrumptious?" Still standing, the resort owner turned to the cook, a handsome young Jamaican man on the other side of the counter, and said, "Fry me up one of those chimis, would you, doll?" Lydia stared at Mrs. Lynx, wondering how someone so utterly beautiful could afford to eat such junk. The woman lightly touched Lydia's arm. "It's Lydia, isn't it?"

"Yes." Lydia was so amazed Mrs. Lynx remembered her name that she didn't know what else to say.

"You're not worried about gaining weight, are you?"

"Uh. Yeah. A bit."

"Tell you what," Mrs. Lynx said, leaning forward and holding Lydia's forearm as if she had a secret, "you go ahead and enjoy a hot chimi, and then come join me in the aerobics class I'm leading this afternoon. Afterward you can sit in the hot tub or get a massage." She winked. "You deserve to pamper yourself a little."

"Can I come?" Ben asked.

Mrs. Lynx laughed as if Ben had made an excellent joke, and Ben smiled a little. "This class is for women only," she said, placing her hand on his shoulder. "We ladies need to work to keep our girlish figures, and we don't want you men around to watch us sweat. But you could go to the weightlifting class. You would enjoy it."

The cook set the chimi in the open spot beside Lydia, but instead of sitting down to eat, Mrs. Lynx pushed the plate in front of Lydia. "You enjoy, sweetheart," she said. She looked right into Lydia's eyes. "Promise me you won't deprive yourself of anything. You're here to enjoy all life has to offer."

Mrs. Lynx walked away. "It's like heaven," Lydia said, her mouth full of spicy meat. "We can do whatever we want."

"Unlike heaven, though," Ben said popping the last of his chimi into his mouth, "this won't last forever." He put his hand on his stomach and groaned in pain.

The aerobics class was easier than Lydia had thought it would be. She didn't even break a sweat. And while getting a massage by a small, quiet brunette, Lydia nearly fell asleep; but then Ben, who was on the table next to hers getting massaged by a short wiry blond man, suggested they go out swimming. "I don't get why people like massages so much," he said as they walked in the sand toward the water. "I think they're boring."

Even Lydia had to agree that playing in the water was much more fun than being pampered. Lydia could have stayed in the sea all afternoon. Whether she was splashing in the waves or floating on her back or diving for shells, she felt perfectly content. Her dad had played some racquetball and was now building a sandcastle on the beach. Mrs. Hinkle was wading in the shore near some rocks, trying to spy the stingray someone had told her about.

Lydia briefly wondered why in the world their taxi driver had seemed to hesitate about this place, but then Ben threw a foam noodle at her, and they began the world's greatest water fight. Soon they were joined by what must have been every kid in the entire resort and even some of the more adventurous adults, Lydia's dad included.

When the water fight, which had turned into a mutated version of Capture the Flag, finally ended almost an hour later, everyone wandered up onto the beach and headed for the resort. But Lydia still couldn't bear to get out of the water. The sun was nearly setting, and the horizon was a stunning red over the blue-green water. Ben stood on the shore, waving her in, but Lydia wasn't ready yet. She dunked her head under water to pull her long hair away from her face. When she surfaced, Ben was waving wildly at her, yelling something she couldn't hear because of the water in her ears. Whatever it was, Ben could wait a few more minutes. Lydia was about to dunk under again when her dad jumped up out of the lawn chair and started running into the water, yelling and waving even more frantically than Ben was.

Lydia shook the water out of her ears, and turned around to see what her dad was pointing to—the fin of a shark just a few feet away.

1
Daddy's Girl

Frank Barnes reached Lydia at the same time the shark did. Lydia felt a jab in her left leg, and then saw her dad's elbow come down hard on the shark's head. "Go!" he yelled at her, and Lydia didn't stop to argue.

When Lydia looked back, her dad—and a pool of blood—were following close behind. "Keep going!" he yelled, catching up to her almost instantly and yanking her forward.

They were in knee-deep water, just within reach of the shore, when the pain in Lydia's leg registered in her brain. She fell down with both hands forward, her face plunging back under the water. In one smooth motion, Frank pulled her out and up into his arms, carrying her onto the shore like a baby. Maybe that's why Lydia began to cry. The beach was nearly empty; all the folks who had been playing all afternoon had gone to hunt down some dinner. Even Hink was nowhere to be seen.

"Get help!" Frank yelled to Ben, whose face had lost all color.

Ben didn't need to be told twice and ran awkwardly through the sand toward the hotel. Frank pulled off his T-shirt and wrapped it tightly around Lydia's wound, whispering words of comfort to her all the while. Lydia, though, just couldn't get herself to stop crying. It wasn't so much that it hurt; it was more that she couldn't get her mind around what had just happened. She had been attacked by a shark!

"You saved me, Daddy!" she said with tears pouring out of her eyes. "You saved me!"

Frank smiled a little and kissed her forehead. "Of course I did, Peachoo. That old shark didn't stand a chance. You'll have to call me the shark slayer from now on."

Lydia smiled through her tears and sat up. "Let me see," she said.

"What?"

"The shark bite. How much did he get?"

Frank gently pulled the T-shirt away from her skin, and immediately the gash started bleeding again, but Lydia had seen enough to know that none of her flesh was missing.

"Nothing a few stitches won't clear up," Frank said, holding the bloody cloth tight against her leg again.

"A few?"

"Fifty, tops," Frank said, with an outright smile now. "Probably forty." He kissed her forehead again. And then again. And then one more time. "Never," he said, holding her face in his hands, "ever do that to me again."

"No, we don't have problems with sharks here," Mrs. Lynx said. "She must have grazed it on the rocks."

Lydia stared at the calm face of the resort owner who was carefully watching the doctor apply the stitches right there at the resort's own medical center. Lydia, shocked by Mrs. Lynx's statement, nearly forgot that she was under the needle. "My dad hit the shark on the head," Lydia said.

Mrs. Lynx laughed. "You're certainly a daddy's girl, aren't you?" She winked at Frank and rested a hand on his arm as if they shared a little joke. "I always made my father out to be a hero too. Enjoy it while you can. It'll pass." She winked again.

Frank didn't crack a smile. "It *was* a shark," he said. "And people have to be warned. Next time it could be worse."

Lydia nodded. The next person might not have an incredible dad like Lydia did. She had to get Mrs. Lynx to believe her. "I saw it, Mrs. Lynx! I saw it with my own eyes."

The resort owner took a step closer to Lydia and her dad. "The last thing folks need," she said in a voice as smooth as ever, "is to have their vacations ruined by an unnecessary attack on their sense of security." Lydia was shocked to see that Mrs. Lynx's eyes revealed a dangerous side.

"*Sense* of security?" Frank exploded. "What about their actual security?"

Mrs. Lynx said nothing, but kept a small smile on her face.

"These stitches will come out on their own," the doctor said to Frank, breaking the silence. "Just be sure she keeps the wound clean. Change the bandage every day for the next couple weeks." He gave Frank a small paper bag full of tape and gauze.

Just before Frank and Lydia walked out the office door, Mrs. Lynx turned to them. "I'd like to offer you a free week here at the resort, and I'd be happy to cover the cost of changing your itinerary with the airline, of course. Only, I trust you will keep the best interest of my patrons in mind, and not terrorize them with fabricated stories—"

"No, thank you," Frank said with a small smile of his own. "And don't worry. I'll tell them nothing but the truth."

They found Ben and Hink waiting outside the door of the clinic, and the four of them headed toward a small café on one of the resort's patios for a late dinner. Lydia could walk now, but she knew that as soon as the numbing medicine wore off, it would hurt to put pressure on that leg.

"You'll do anything to get out of schoolwork, won't you, young lady," Hink said without smiling as they seated themselves around a small square table under the evening sky. They had been planning to begin lessons right after dinner.

"Uh," Lydia grunted before she realized the tutor was joking.

"I think she was trying to cut out some extra pounds," Frank said, winking. He still looked a bit tense, though.

Ben laughed. "I think she was just looking for a way to stay here at the resort longer."

If the last idea had been her plan, it immediately backfired. Ms. Young, the young Jamaican woman who had registered them, headed for their table. She lowered her eyes and said, "Sah. Ladies. My deepest apologies for de inconvenience, but the room you had hoped to arrange for another night is no longer available. My mistress asks that you accept her apology by receiving a full reimbursement for your stay with us—and enjoy dis last meal with her compliments. I escort you from de premises."

To say that Frank was mad would be like saying Jamaicans like Bob Marley or that getting lost on the back roads of Jamaica was a bad idea. The four ex-vacationers were now someplace far from the Luxury Resort, racing along on the northwest part of the island in the 4Runner Hink had rented. It was dark, they seemed to be lost, and yes, Frank was mad.

Lydia was in the backseat behind her dad, trying to pretend her leg didn't hurt and that the bandage wasn't getting redder by the moment. Ben was snoozing beside her, somehow tuning out the fighting up front. Hink was barking out regular orders to Frank, with Frank growling back. Literally. From where Lydia was sitting, she couldn't see whether his ears were pulled back and his teeth were bared, but she wouldn't have been surprised. The coast had been somewhere to their left for the first few miles on the main road, but now her dad had turned right onto a small dirt road heading straight into the jungle.

"Stop, Frank!" Mrs. Hinkle demanded, her voice high and sharp. "We must figure out where we are."

"May I remind you, Gretchen, that we are following precise directions from my GPS?" Frank said, not exactly sweetly. "I'm not lost. We'll be out in the boonies here for several miles, so just relax."

"Dad?" Lydia said.

"Yes, honey," he said in not quite a growl.

Lydia felt bad for adding more stress to his life, but knew she needed to deal with her little problem; the blood was starting to drip down her leg. "I think I need another bandage. And maybe a painkiller."

That did get him to stop the car. "Oh, my baby," he said, his mood radically changed. The stress was still there, but it had transformed from anger to compassion. "Let me see." The car was still running and the headlights shone along the side of the road and into the forest beyond the curve. Frank unbuckled and leaned back over the seat. "Oh, my baby," he said again as soon as he saw the blood. "I'll get the first-aid kit." He had put the bandage supplies the doctor had given him in the first-aid kit he had packed back home. It was a small duffel bag full of emergency medical supplies, including prescription antibiotics, sterile bandages, antibiotic wipes, burn ointment, eyewash solution, tweezers, and over-the-counter drugs. Lydia had been sure they wouldn't need any of the stuff and that they were wasting space, but now she was glad her dad had been so thorough.

Frank opened the door and stepped into the blackness. Ben woke up and looked around. "What's going on?" he mumbled.

"I just hope there are no wild animals out there," Hink said sourly as Frank rummaged through the trunk.

Ben and Lydia looked at each other for a moment, and then Lydia called, "Dad! I'm okay. Come back in!"

He didn't come back in. Instead he opened Lydia's door and gently turned her toward him. Hink harrumphed, but Frank paid no attention. He handed Lydia a large white gel pill and a bottle of water. She stared at him. Since when did she swallow pills the size of footballs? With water? She could hardly swallow little decongestants without a large glass of Sunny Delight. But her dad didn't notice her stress. He placed a towel under her leg and slowly pulled the blood-soaked bandage off, his back to the darkness.

Lydia closed her eyes and threw the pill down her throat before she could think about it any longer. It didn't work. She gagged it back up.

"You okay, Peachoo?" her dad asked, barely glancing up from his work.

Ben leaned over to get a better look at what Frank was doing. The overhead light was dim, but it was enough for him to see what he was looking for. "That's a lot of stitches, Lyd!"

Frank laughed for the first time since they got kicked out of the Luxury Resort. He was happiest when he was fixing a problem. "You bet, Ben. Our girl earned herself a thirty-seven-stitch war wound." He cleaned the blood from her leg with a wipe and pressed a fresh bandage on the lightly bleeding wound. "You ought to be proud, Lyd!" He winked at Lydia, who was watching him wrap the white medical tape tightly around her leg, holding the new bandage firmly in place.

Lydia didn't answer either of them. She was trying to psych herself up to try swallowing the pill again. She needed to get rid of this pain somehow.

"That was one aggressive rock," Ben said, grinning. He held his fingers up to indicate quote marks when he said "rock."

Frank laughed harshly and then shook his head. "That woman . . ." His voice trailed off and Lydia worried that he would go back to being grumpy. Instead, he chuckled and turned to Mrs. Hinkle. "I think we've found your match, Hink," he said.

Lydia expected Mrs. Hinkle to puff up like a threatened cat, but instead her scowl fell off and was replaced by an upward turn of her thin red lips. "Ha!" she said, which was as close to a laugh as one could hope for from her.

Frank didn't seem to be as scared of the darkness—or more accurately, the creatures in the darkness—as Lydia was. He took his sweet old time cleaning up the mess. Lydia figured she'd better get this pill down before they started driving again. She threw the pill into the back of her mouth and poured water after it. The water slid down her throat, but the pill just wouldn't follow. It was like little workers were throwing rope around her teeth to stop the pill from rushing down the waterfall.

"Are we going to warn the resort guests about the shark?" Ben asked.

Frank sighed heavily and gently turned Lydia's legs away from the door. "I don't know, Ben. I don't know." He closed the door, put the duffel away, and got back into the driver's seat. Lydia breathed a sigh of relief. No wild animal had attacked. Things were looking up.

"Of course we're going to do something about it," Hink said.

Frank pulled back onto the deserted road and made a sharp left at the bend.

Hink continued. "We're going inform the authorities—"

"Gretchen," Frank said with a warning tone in his voice.

"But, Dad! It would be educational!" Lydia said, surprised to find herself defending Hink. She gave up on taking the painkiller. Capping the water bottle, she dropped the pill in her pocket. A little bit of pain never hurt anyone.

"Yeah. Wouldn't that be like a government class or something?" Ben asked.

"What is our primary purpose in coming here?" Frank asked, slowing down as an old white sign appeared in the distance. Mrs. Hinkle strained forward as if trying to read it before he did. "To further your education or to minister to the people?"

"We would be ministering to all those people on the beach who are about to get mauled by sharks!" Lydia said. She pointed to her left leg even though no one could see it in the darkness. It was throbbing now, and she almost wished the shark had pulled the whole thing off.

"What is our primary purpose in coming here?" Frank asked again. "To pamper the rich Americans and Europeans who use this island as a private playground or to minister to the poverty-stricken villagers they are stealing from?"

"Stealing from?" Lydia, Mrs. Hinkle, and Ben all asked at once.

Frank clicked on his high beams as they rolled out of the forest and continued following the road through dark fields. "Yes," he said. "Stealing."

"How are they stealing?" Ben asked. Lydia would have asked herself, but her leg hurt too much to talk.

"Do you think we could have afforded to stay at the Luxury Resort if we were not stealing?" Frank asked. No one said anything, and he continued. "Yesterday I tried not to think of it this way. I convinced myself that we were providing work for the Jamaicans. But just wait. You'll see."

5
In the Jungle

After they drove slowly for another ten minutes on the dirt road, turning right and then left, the headlights of the SUV suddenly swept onto one home and then another. It was still dark, so Lydia couldn't see much, but the homes they continued to pass seemed to be the size of the shed in Lydia's backyard in Indy. From the lights of the vehicle, Lydia could see the shacks had no windows and were messily thrown together with some sort of sheet metal. She could see vague outlines of similar buildings in the darkness beyond.

People were out walking, and Frank drove slowly, smiling as he passed the waving residents. He stopped at a larger dirt road and waited for another car to pass, and then drove on. Soon the crowd began to thin and the houses spread farther apart.

When he turned right, clearly heading out of "town," if that's what the collection of huts could be called, Mrs. Hinkle spoke up. "Do you really expect me to believe that you know where you're going?"

"I sure do," Frank said. "We're almost there."

Sure enough, less than ten minutes later, after passing through another batch of trees, Frank rolled to a stop next to a building that was bigger than all the houses. Lydia didn't get to look around because right away a small crowd of men, women, and children were waving and laughing and jumping up and down—some of them covering their eyes with their hands to block the glare of the headlights.

"Were they expecting us?" Mrs. Hinkle asked quietly.

"They knew we'd be here sometime this month," Frank said.

When Frank turned out the lights, Lydia thought she had suddenly gone blind. She looked up and saw some stars, but most were covered by clouds. She could just imagine how huge that sky must look when the clouds were gone.

"Welcome, welcome!" a woman said in the familiar Jamaican accent as soon as Frank stepped out of the car.

"We welcome you to our home," another person said, a man this time. "And we tank you for coming. Praise de Lord!"

Lydia blinked a few times, and slowly she was able to make out shapes and figures. Her leg felt sore and stiff, and she really didn't feel like moving.

"Thank you!" Frank said. "We're so glad to be here!"

Lydia opened the door and carefully shifted her leg so she could step out of the car on the other leg. She didn't want to be rude. Ben and Hink were already by her dad's side. Lydia managed to smile as she walked up, and was quickly pulled into hugs by their hosts. She tried to keep smiling, but she worried that all that moving was making her leg bleed again. After a few minutes, she hobbled back to the car and sat sideways in the backseat with the door open and her feet on the running board.

"What be wrong wit' you?" a boy asked. From the interior light of the truck, Lydia could see he looked to be about twelve, but he was short for his age. That didn't stop him from being confident. He had a secret little smile on his face, as if he knew he'd won a trophy but no one else knew it yet. His hair was cut short, but his eyebrows were thick and messy. "Can you not walk?"

"I can some," Lydia said. She held up her leg and the white bandage glowed in the light. "I hurt my leg today, but it should be better soon."

Ben saw them talking and slipped away from the adults too. He leaned up against the truck next to Lydia. A few more kids followed him, and a semicircle formed around Ben and Lydia.

"What happen?" a girl asked. She looked to be about the same age as the boy. She had his same confidence, though the boy looked as if he couldn't wait for others to find out what he was gloating about and she looked like she'd rather no one would notice her latest achievement.

Lydia didn't want to say that she was attacked by a shark because it sounded so . . . bizarre. She didn't think anyone would believe her, anyway. "Just a gash," she said. "It'll be alright."

"She got attacked by a shark," Ben said.

"You lucky to be alive," the first boy said. He didn't seem a bit surprised to hear of the attack.

"Her dad saved her," Ben said, pointing with his head toward Frank. "He jumped into the water and knocked the shark on the head with his elbow."

"Whoa!" said many of the kids at once. They all looked at Frank with something like reverence in their eyes.

"I be Melvin," the first boy said to Lydia, holding out his hand. Lydia shook it and smiled. "Lydia," she said.

"I be Jillisa, Melvin's sistah," the girl said.

"Twin sistah," Melvin said. He grinned and put his arm around Jillisa, as if to get a reaction from Lydia about how much they looked alike, but it was too dark for Lydia to be able to tell anyone apart.

"Cool," Lydia said.

The kids filed up and shook Lydia's hand and told their names, and then did the same to Ben.

Lydia wondered how long she would have to sit there smiling through her pain, when her dad took his leave from the adults and headed over to Lydia. The kids parted a path for him, all staring up at the shark slayer. "How are you doing, Lydia?" he asked, gesturing toward her leg.

"It hurts."

"The painkiller hasn't kicked in yet?" He ignored the kids who stood back just a bit, watching their every move.

Lydia shrugged. "I can't . . . uh . . . swallow it." She said it very quietly so no one would hear.

Frank looked at her for a second, as if waiting for her to correct herself. When she didn't, he laughed. "Mind over matter, kid," he said. "I can't do this for you. It's all up to you."

"I know," Lydia said. "I'll be okay."

Lydia was relieved to go to bed, even though bed was the backseat of the 4Runner. Ben curled up in the rear hatch on top of the luggage. Each of them had brought one or two suitcases or packs plus carry-on bags, but Ben arranged it all to be fairly flat, and then threw his pillow and blanket on top of it all. The adults reclined in the front seats. Lydia's dad had pulled mosquito netting from somewhere and covered up the opened windows. "Believe it or not, this is much more comfortable than sleeping in one of their homes," he said. "It's very hot in there."

Lydia didn't say anything. She had used up all her energy being polite to the villagers, and now she just wanted to cry. No matter what position she put herself in, she couldn't get comfortable, couldn't make the pain stop. Part of her was glad her dad was not babying her, but another part wanted him to kiss it all away.

Sometime in the middle of the night Lydia woke to a wild, unearthly shriek followed by numbing silence. Everyone else remained sleeping, and Lydia started to wonder if she had done the shrieking herself. Her leg was in miserable pain.

"I'm going to do it," she whispered. She snatched up the water bottle and pulled the pill from her pocket. "I'm going to do it." She popped the pill in her mouth, spilled water after it, and then smiled as she felt the lump slide down her throat. Weird how easy that was when just a few hours before it had been impossible.

A half hour later, during which time she heard another shriek that was most definitely not coming from her own mouth but from some jungle creature, the pain subsided and Lydia fell asleep.

Lydia woke up to an early morning light looking for a bathroom. Frank directed her to a tree instead. "I'm sure they have an outhouse, but this will work just fine for now," her dad said. As angry as she was with Mrs. Lynx, Lydia couldn't help thinking about the luxurious room and lavish breakfast back at the resort.

By the look on Ben's face when Lydia limped back, he was feeling the same way.

Mrs. Hinkle groaned loudly as she got out of the car, and Lydia thought she might say something like, "I'm getting too old for this." Instead, the old woman said, "I can't believe I forgot my tree climbers. They'd be perfect here."

Lydia tried not to imagine the old woman in spiked shoes climbing up a tree like a beetle. Instead she looked around at their surroundings. They were parked at the side of the road in the middle of a clearing, the jungle looming up all around them. Lydia didn't think she had ever seen so many different shades of green or types of trees—from large-leafed banana trees to gray mahogany trees to spidery papaya trees. To their left and to their right, just a few miles away in both directions, were green mountains.

They were parked at a fork in the road. On one side of the road they had been driving on was a huge garden with a banana field on the far end; on the other side were about ten huts like the one Lydia had noticed last night, some better constructed than others. More homes were scattered on either side of the road past the fork plus down the other road. These places didn't look as ramshackle as some of the neighborhoods that Lydia had seen in Liberia, but it was not close to being suburban Indianapolis either.

The 4Runner was parked next to a hand-pumped well and the only large building in sight. The building was the size of the pavilion at the park by Lydia's old house, and structured much the same. White painted beams in each corner and in the middle of each side held up a thatched roof, and eight white painted picnic tables were placed in two rows inside. At one end of the pavilion was a chalkboard and podium.

"That's the school," Frank said. "GRO has been supporting this school financially, but we haven't been able to get anyone out here yet to check it out." He shook his head. "I can see already that we need to invest some money here. We need to build a place with walls."

"Ah, school," said Hink, rubbing her hands together and smiling wickedly at Ben and Lydia. "We should have fun here, kids. No more frivolities to distract us. Just you, me, and Shakespeare."

Frank grinned, clearly back on good terms with the tutor, much to Lydia's dismay. She had been hoping to wiggle her way out of lessons this week. "Yes," he said. "You both have exams when we return to the States—to be administered by our own Mrs. Hinkle."

"Exams! Dad! I thought—"

"You thought you were supposed to take them two weeks ago?" he asked. "I know. I'm so sorry. We're running a little behind schedule." His overdramatic voice showed that he probably thought he was funny.

"I hope," Hink said to Lydia, no humor in her voice at all, "that you remember the algebra we studied in Liberia. We will take that exam first. And you have, of course, been keeping up with the other courses since you left? You will be tested on those too."

Lydia had been studying hard, but for some reason didn't want to admit that to her teacher.

She didn't have to, because just then a woman—the same one who had been first to welcome them last night—walked toward them, her arms outstretched. "Come, Mr. Barnes," she said. "Come all. We make breakfast for you. We make for you our national favorite."

Lydia thought of the national favorite in Liberia—foufou, weird stuff that looked like slimy snot. Lydia had refused to eat the foufou that was offered to her and nearly lost the hidden treasure because of it. Not this time. She'd eat the Jamaican "national favorite" even if it killed her.

6
No Barrel of Laughs

Breakfast in rural Jamaica was entirely different than breakfast in a Jamaican resort, except for one thing. Both were delicious. Instead of sitting in cushioned chairs by the coast being waited on by five-star servers, Lydia was sitting on a woven mat, squished in a tight circle around a low table, reaching and grabbing for her food. She was sitting between Ben and her dad. Mrs. Hinkle sat on the other side of her dad.

It seemed that all the residents within sight had come for breakfast, including the kids Lydia and Ben had met last night. Jillisa and Melvin sat next to each other—with Jillisa next to Ben—arm-in-arm, talking a mile a minute to each other. Most of the other kids had ratty clothes, but Jillisa wore a cute tank top with matching shorts and Melvin had crisp tan shorts and a clean black shirt. And it was now very clear to Lydia that they were twins. They had the same huge smile and small, round nose in an oval face. What was striking, though, was how similar they could look while still being clearly all boy and all girl. If they were to be cast in *The Lord of the Rings*, Melvin would be a boy version of Strider—tough and wild; Jillisa would be an elf—beautiful and pure. Both were strong and good.

"What is this stuff, Dad?" Lydia whispered after taking a bite of something that looked like scrambled eggs but tasted rich and nutty. "It's awesome!"

Frank looked up at their host, Mrs. Young, who was sitting next to Hink. Mrs. Young smiled. "Ackee and salt fish," she said. She pointed to a bushel of red tropical fruit just out of reach behind Lydia. "That is ackee, the national fruit of Jamaica."

Lydia leaned back to reach for one, but Jillisa grabbed Lydia's arm. "D'ose not be ripe," she said. "Eat d'ose only that have been opened and de seeds removed."

"De seeds, dey kill you," Melvin added.

Lydia didn't believe it for a second, but she sat forward anyway.

Mrs. Young nodded. "Yes, if ackee be forced open before it be ripe, it is poison."

"Strong enough to kill?" Frank asked.

"Yes, if it be eaten."

Ben whistled between his teeth and pushed his plate away.

"No, mon, it be good now," Jillisa said, laughing. "Here." She dashed off and came back with a piece of the fruit that looked like it had burst open. Inside was a soft, mild, creamy, yellowish flesh and big black seeds. "See," she said. "Only de seeds be poison. When it bust open on its own, we remove de seeds."

"And what is this dish?" Hink asked, scooping out a large serving of dark green soup.

"Callaloo," Melvin said. "It be made from that." He pointed to some plants with big oval leaves and delicate red blossoms growing beside the road.

Hink slurped down the soup loudly and then sighed deeply with her eyes closed. "Mmmm."

If Lydia hadn't seen this same I-love-all-things-foreign behavior from her teacher in Africa, she would have thought the woman had finally found home.

Mrs. Young smiled and patted Hink appreciatively. "You be one of us, Mrs. Hinkle. You be one of us."

The two women began talking education. Mrs. Young was serving as the teacher at the school. Lydia quickly started up her own conversation with Jillisa, hoping to postpone the whole classroom thing for as long as possible. "So, which one is your mom?" she asked, scanning the crowd, trying to figure out which woman looked most like the twins.

"None of dem," Jillisa said. "Our mother be living in Florida."

"Florida?"

"Yes, and our father too." Jillisa lifted her head high and said, "And dey be calling for us soon. Mel and me, we become American citizens."

But Melvin shoved her with his elbow. "Don't be lying," he said quietly. "You know that will never happen."

"It will!" Jillisa glared at him before turning back to Lydia. "Mother send us a package every two weeks, and you should see de tings she give us." She held up her arm and showed off the fifty or so rubber bracelets of all different colors. "Plus she send candy. And clothes. And soap. And shoes. Dey be waiting to get de papers straight, and den dey gonna send for us."

But Melvin jumped up, messing up the woven mat. "What parents ever be coming back for de kids?" he asked loudly. "We be barrel children, Jilly, and we be so always!" He ran off toward the schoolhouse, and everyone was quiet.

"What are barrel children?" Lydia asked her dad as they walked slowly back to the 4Runner to gather up school supplies. Ben and Hink were already there. Hink was trying to pull out a hard green suitcase from the back of the vehicle, and Ben was catching the stuff that was falling out as she tugged. The ladies were cleaning up the breakfast and the men were getting ready to head out to the fields, gathering up rakes and hoes and wheelbarrows. The women would soon join them.

"I think you got the idea of what barrel children are," Frank said quietly. "They are kids who get left behind with relatives while parents go out to wealthier countries to try to make a better situation for their families. They're called barrel children because their parents send back barrels full of stuff."

"So do the parents ever come back?"

Frank held his palms up and shrugged. "Each situation is different, of course. But often they don't."

Lydia felt sick. She thought of her dad, who couldn't stand it when Lydia was out of his sight for even a few hours. And she thought of Arway, a woman she met in Africa, who had searched for years for her missing daughter. She thought of Mitri, her friend in Palestine, whose father drove past dangerous checkpoints every day to see his son. How could parents actually choose to be away from their kids? "Why don't they come back?"

"They are too poor. They think going to America or Europe is like going to the land of milk and honey, but when they arrive, they are even more poor than they were here."

Lydia looked around. The poverty in rural Jamaica was severe. The homes looked like they would blow away in the wind. There was no electricity, no running water, no suitable clothing.

"Here, even without money," Frank continued, "they have food. Remember, they are farmers. And, of course, they have the great wealth of being part of a community. When they go off to other countries, they may gain a bit more cash, but often not enough to buy a better home or food to feed their families."

"Wow." Lydia didn't know what to say. Melvin could be right about his parents never coming back for them. Lydia couldn't imagine how much that would hurt, and she didn't blame Jillisa for denying it. Lydia would have had to keep hoping too, just to be able to survive.

Lydia and her dad had arrived at the car now, and Mrs. Hinkle had freed the suitcase and was now digging for more stuff. "Here, you take this, Lydia," Mrs. Hinkle said. "I think I have a few other things in here that may help. Now let me see . . ."

Lydia didn't listen. The old lady was basically talking to herself anyway, and Lydia had too much on her mind.

A few minutes later the four Americans went into the schoolhouse where the kids were clustered in little groups, some talking, others playing marbles with pebbles in the sand, others playing tag. Melvin and Jillisa were chatting happily in the far corner, as if Melvin hadn't had an outburst a half hour earlier. They were teasing a younger girl, about the age of nine, who was without a doubt their sister.

Mrs. Hinkle went to Mrs. Young and began showing her the materials she had brought. The two women continued the conversation they had begun at breakfast about their teaching plan for the next week. Frank went to one of the beams and pushed on it, checking its stability. Ben and Lydia went over to Jillisa and Melvin.

"Ah, you so pretty," the little sister said to Lydia.

Lydia smiled, but she felt less excited about the compliment than she would have yesterday—before she met the beautiful and evil Mrs. Lynx. "Thank you. What's your name?"

"Sophia."

"Hi, Sophia. I'm Lydia, and this is Ben. You must be Melvin and Jillisa's sister."

"Wow!" Sophia said. "You be smart and pretty!"

Lydia laughed. Now that was a compliment! "So do you have other brothers and sisters, or is it just the three of you?"

Jillisa wrapped her arms around her little sister. "We have one big sistah."

"She's our half-sistah really," Melvin said.

"She be Marcy," Sophia said. "She be twenty-one and she work at de resort."

Jillisa's smile turned suddenly to a grimace. "I wish she don't."

"Really? Why?" Lydia asked.

"She should be here with us," Jillisa said.

"Plus, her boss be a crook," Melvin said.

Ben snorted. They knew all about lousy resort owners. "She doesn't work at the Luxury Resort, does she?"

"Yeah, mon!" Melvin said. "She do! How do you know?"

Lydia could hardly believe it. "You've got to be kidding! We stayed there for a night."

"Yeah, and we met her boss," Ben said.

Lydia nodded and said quietly, "That woman is worse than a crook."

Ben told the story of the shark attack and how Mrs. Lynx had quickly gotten rid of them.

"What it be like at de Luxury Resort?" Melvin asked.

"Haven't you been there?" Lydia asked.

Melvin looked at her as if she had just asked if he had ever turned into a cat.

"Well," Lydia said, "I just thought you might have gone to see your sister."

"We not be allowed there. And Marcy not be allowed to leave," Sophia said, as bitterly as her brother.

"Not allowed to leave?" Lydia asked.

"No, mon. She be workin' all de time or she lose her job."

"But can't she come home on weekends or whatever?" Ben asked.

"No, mon. She be workin' all de time," Melvin said, as if Ben hadn't heard the first time.

"She do get two weekends off each year," Jillisa said. "That's when she brings us our packages from our mother and father."

"Does she live at the resort?" Lydia asked.

"No. She live with our cousin's family at a house nearby," Jillisa said. "She not be there much, though. She workin' most de time."

"Maybe we saw her," Ben said. "How weird."

"I'd hate to work there," Lydia said. "I can't stand Mrs. Lynx." Her leg wasn't feeling as terrible as it had yesterday, mostly because she was able to take her medicine now, but somehow the injury seemed to be all Mrs. Lynx's fault.

"Why doesn't Marcy get a different job?" Ben asked.

"What else can she do?" Melvin asked. "She can't read, so she can't get no government job. Granny don't want her to farm. No future in that."

"She can't read?" Ben asked.

"'Course not," Jillisa said. "Dis school be starting only two years ago, and she be workin' by den."

"You didn't go to school until two years ago?" Ben asked. Lydia wanted to hit him. He sounded like a parent talking about popular music, knowing nothing and asking all the wrong questions.

"I know nutting about no school until Ms. Young come," Melvin said. "I didn't even know what readin' was."

Lydia forgot about Ben being a dope and stared at Melvin like he had just said he didn't know what toothpaste was, and then she wondered if he didn't know what toothpaste was. "Oh," she said.

"Come, children," Mrs. Young said—and the kids ran in from all directions and sat on the picnic table benches. Jillisa and Melvin took their seats near the back of the classroom, tugging Ben and Lydia along with them. Sophia ran to join her friends up front.

"As you see," Mrs. Young said as soon as everyone had settled down, "we have new students and a new teacher with us. Dey be here for just one week, so please make dem very welcome."

"Why dey be here?" a little girl up front whispered loudly to the teacher, as if she hoped no one else would hear her.

Laughter erupted and Mrs. Young quickly said, "Good question." She waited for a hush and then said, "These wonderful people, including Mr. Barnes in de back"—and all the kids turned in their seats to stare at Frank, who was standing among a bunch of the other adults who had come to watch—"are part of de organization that send me to start de school—" The rest of her words were cut off by the applause.

"Tank you!" a woman beside her finally said over the noisy crowd. "You give us new hope, hope for de children."

Amen to that! With an education, maybe Jillisa and Melvin wouldn't wind up being slaves to the likes of Mrs. Lynx. It was enough to make Lydia want to stand up and cheer herself. And she would have if Mrs. Lynx's pet shark hadn't tried to make a meal of her leg.

Once class was in session, Lydia turned to her dad. "Can't I help teach?" She put as much passion in her voice as she could muster. "They need me!" She couldn't help noticing that the students around her, even the older ones like Melvin and Jillisa, were still reading Dick and Jane books, like from the 1950s. And there she was with Shakespeare on her lap. She felt bad.

"You need to do your own work, Peachoo," her dad said. "If you finish up the assignment Hink gave you before the school day is over, then you can help." He grabbed her arm before she went whooping back to her seat. "*If,*" he said, "it's okay with the teachers. I'll talk to them."

Lydia went straight to work. She knew how to work hard and fast. She'd been doing the same thing at home for the last two weeks—finishing up as quickly as possible so she'd have time to chat with her friends online and download music. It turned out that the boy she met in Israel, Marcus, liked a lot of the same music she did.

"Work!" Ben whispered to her, and Lydia jumped. Oops. She'd slipped into daydreaming already.

Focus. Focus. Focus.

But she couldn't focus long. About a half hour after she had stuck her nose into *Much Ado about Nothing*, she heard the most surprising sound.

7

Tour Gone Bad

It might have been the sound of heavy rain pounding against a tent roof, except that the sun was shining brightly. Lydia lifted her head and looked down the road. Others were staring too, but none of the others looked confused. Some glanced up at the teacher as if dreading her reaction.

Sure enough, Mrs. Young lifted her head from Sophia's desk where she had been helping. Just at that moment, Lydia saw about twenty horseback riders break out of the jungle and enter the small town. She could hear the high-pitched voice of the British tour guide above the clip-clopping of the horses' hooves.

"And to your right you see a typical Jamaican village, where the children are hard at work at school and the mums and dads are out working the crops. It's a good life here in rural Jamaica, a life that many of you would covet: a place where you can forget the rat race and instead pursue the simple pleasure of an honest day's work."

The people smiled at the tour guide and smiled at the kids. Lydia wanted to throw ackee fruit at them—the guide made it sound like life was so easy.

"To your left you'll notice the crops that the villagers are growing. Banana trees are—"

Mrs. Young walked to the edge of the schoolhouse and put her hands on her hips. "Excuse I," she said.

"Oh!" the guide said, clearly startled. "Oh, pardon me!" He stopped where he was, and Lydia chuckled. Mrs. Young was a Jamaican version of Hink.

"If you be so sure life is sweet here, why don' we do a little switch?" Mrs. Young said. "You stay here for one day. Den your children be makin' our breakfast, and you be washin' our clothes. Den we ride in on our fine horses and gape at you!"

The horses bunched up in the middle of the street, and the tourists looked worried. "Oh, I say!" the guide said, letting his eyes flit in every direction, as if looking for an escape.

"Maybe you trouble to find out what life be like here before you tell all these people how wonderful it be," Mrs. Young said. "Why don' you give dem a real tour?"

Hink and Frank moved from the middle of the classroom to stand beside Mrs. Young. The kids too, with Lydia leading the charge, leapt from their seats and ran to the edge of the classroom to watch.

The tourists noticed the white folk for the first time and seemed relieved. "Yes, well, hello," the guide said to Frank. "I'm sure there has been a misunderstanding." He looked at Mrs. Hinkle, who probably looked like a sweet old lady to him, with a hopeful smile on his face.

But when Hink said, "Yes, we can work that out; why don't you get off your high horse and find out what you're talking about?" his smile slipped off and fell smack into the dirt.

That's when Lydia's dad took over. "Of course it's just a mis-understanding," he said, picking up the smile and putting it on himself. He walked out of the schoolhouse to stand below the guide, looking very small under the giant horse. He didn't look a bit scared, though. "Why don't you stay for a short visit just to clear the air?"

The guide hesitated, but the man behind him said in a British accent, "Pardon me, aren't you Frank Barnes?"

Frank looked over at the man. He was a jolly chap with a big gut and red cheeks. "Tom Adams! Good to see you again. You folks are from the Luxury Resort, then?"

They all nodded as if that detail freed them from all awk-wardness. "Frank is from Global Relief and Outreach," the man said to the woman beside him, and she made a big O with her mouth, nodding politely. "Plus he entirely squashed me in a game of racquetball back at the resort," the man said, grin-ning. He turned back to Frank. "So, what are you doing out here?"

"We came to check on the school GRO set up here." Frank gestured to include all of the schoolhouse. "It's the only school for miles around—"

"Well," the guide said. "There's an excellent school in Grange Hill, of course—"

"Which be ten miles from here," Mrs. Young said, moving to stand next to Frank. "And as you see, we have no horses to ride." She turned to Tom. "Dis guide take tourists through de village every day, He make you rich folk think it be alright, what you doin.'"

"Right. Let's move on, then!" the guide yelled and urged his horse forward.

"Just because we be de only village with a bit of hope," Mrs. Young continued loudly, "you bring dem here and make dem feel alright." The tourists began to file along after the guide. "I dare you!" she yelled after them. "You take dem horses a few miles down de road where de kids don' have a school, where everybody be so poor the smell will slap you in the face, where dey have no parents—no hope!" Her voice got louder as they moved away.

Tom had let the others file past him as he stayed next to Frank. Even the woman he was with moved on. "Is this true, Frank?" Tom asked.

Lydia's dad lowered his head and nodded. "It's all true."

"And this school is really making a difference?"

"Yes, by the grace of God," Frank said.

"Well, you know I can't get them all to stay for a visit, but I'll do what I can to generate a little interest back at the resort."

"How?" Hink asked. She was still standing up at the school with the kids.

"Yes, how?" Mrs. Young asked. Tom hadn't addressed the teacher once.

"I don't know," Tom said. "I'll talk to some others and see if they want to come out here for an afternoon and help out or something."

"That's a great idea, Tom," Frank said.

"No one will come," Hink muttered under her breath, just loud enough for Lydia to hear. Then she called out to Tom,

"Maybe you could get folks to give up one day of meals and let one of the villagers eat in their place that day."

"Yes!" Lydia said. It was a great idea. "I'll come with you and help you get people excited about this!"

"No," Frank said. "You're not going back there." He turned to Tom. "Thanks for sticking around, Tom. Do what you can."

Tom rode off, and everyone settled back into their seats.

Hink quickly brought the class back to order and began teaching again. But moments later the sound of horse hooves beating the path could be heard above Hink's nasally voice.

Frank went quickly to the edge of the classroom to see what was going on.

"Have a care about what you are doing!" the tour guide called to Frank after swinging his horse around to face the direction he had just come from. He lifted one finger and pointed it at Frank. "You just watch yourself," he said again. "My boss is not going to like this."

He kicked his heels into the horse's sides. And then he was gone.

The tour guide's boss was the last thing on Lydia's mind when she went to bed that night. Or to the backseat of the truck. Whatever. She was thinking about the stars, which she was staring at through the mosquito-netting window. With no electricity and no wireless connection here in the backcountry, she couldn't

IM Marcus or write on her blog, but the darkness meant she could see the sky in a way she never had before. She wondered if God put the stars carefully into place like a puzzle or if he rolled them out of his hands like marbles and let them spread out in the heavens to wherever they happened to land. Or maybe he could talk to the stars. Would he have told each star exactly where to go, or would he have let it choose its own location?

Lydia was glad everyone else was sleeping, so she could enjoy this quiet time. Her dad's breathing was deep and steady; Hink's was squeaky and uneven; Ben's was nearly silent. He must have been sleeping better tonight since he took all the luggage out to make room for his lanky legs. He was almost as tall as Lydia now.

Lydia's neck was starting to ache from staring up at the sky, but she was worried shifting positions might wake someone up— or hurt her leg, which was now blissfully pain free.

As she was deciding what to do, Lydia heard scuffling outside. She sat up quickly and tried to see who was out there. She could make out shadows by the schoolhouse and heard low voices. When she saw flames, she considered getting out of the truck to join the campfire, but then she saw more flames a few feet away, and then some more.

"Dad!" she whispered loudly, and he snorted. "Dad, wake up. Something's wrong."

He woke up and looked around. His eyes landed on the flames and he stared at them for just a moment before they seemed to register. "Hey!" he suddenly yelled. "Hey!"

Frank yanked open the door and left it open as he ran toward the fire makers. Lydia started to follow him but didn't get far; Hink came up behind Lydia and pulled her to the side under the shadow of a tree. "Stay here," Hink whispered. When Ben walked up looking very confused, Hink pointed him to Lydia with her chin and said again, "Stay there."

Lydia could hear her dad yelling, but she couldn't see him. Then, to her horror, the darkness of the night disappeared as the three or four small fires she had spotted licked up the sides of the schoolhouse. The sudden brightness revealed the silhouette of her dad wrestling with another, larger silhouette. Lydia could see Hink running toward them, and then other people appeared out of nowhere; but the large shadow her dad was grappling with lifted a powerful arm and dropped it on her dad's shoulder before anyone could make it to them.

"Dad!" Lydia screamed, not even remembering that Hink had told her to stay. "Dad!"

8
Dragon Slayer

Frank was struggling to his feet by the time Lydia reached him. He was swatting Mrs. Hinkle away and yelling, "Let me go! Let me get them!"

Hink, though, was not letting him go. She had both hands under his left elbow, and was trying to help him up—and holding him back from running off after the man who had just knocked him down. Lydia grabbed the other arm.

"Daddy!" she said. "Stay here! Please."

Some villagers were running after the man who had attacked her dad, and others were trying to put out the fire. When Ben arrived, Hink released Frank and he took a few steps toward the schoolhouse. Lydia followed. They wouldn't be able to put the fire out before the building collapsed, she knew. Even Frank seemed to realize that. He slowed down and held the shoulder that had been struck, and stood staring at the flames, which now covered the entire building. Bits of the thatched roof were falling down into the middle of the classroom and setting the picnic tables on fire.

"Mr. Barnes!" Ben yelled. He was pointing toward the 4Runner.

Lydia and her dad turned in time to see the lights of the vehicle flood over them and then disappear around a corner. Some of the villagers ran after it, shouting, but Frank just stood there, staring.

"This is not good," he said quietly. He took one step toward the men who were chasing the vehicle, and then he turned back to the fire.

"You stay away!" Lydia's dad said to her, walking backward. "And I mean it!" He pointed a finger at her for one long second, and then went on.

Lydia obeyed. She watched her dad jog toward the others who were fighting the orange monster that had eaten the school and was now threatening to lick up the nearby houses. Jillisa was at the water pump, her arms moving the lever up and down as fast as she could; adults filled up buckets and threw the water at the fire. It was useless. The water fell on the flames with as much force as a twig against a brick wall.

"Mr. Barnes!" a voice yelled. It was Ben. "Over here. Help me with this!" Ben was trying to fill his little arms with burlap sacks that were in a large pile beside the gardens on the other side of the road. "Let's get these wet!" he hollered.

Frank promptly turned around. He didn't say anything like "Good job!" or "Excellent idea," but his jaw tightened and his head lifted a bit. Lydia knew Ben had given her dad a fresh dose of hope. She ran over to help. Here was a way she could help without going near the fire.

Others caught on to the idea and began piling the sacks under the water pump. Jillisa and Lydia took turns pumping the water as fast as they could to soak the burlap. Frank grabbed the first one and headed straight for the place where the fire was forming into what looked to Lydia like the face of a giant dragon. He flung the burlap sack straight into its mouth.

At first nothing happened, but then the bag hit a beam that had not yet fallen—and stuck. A black rectangle replaced the flames in that spot for a moment, and soon fifty other black rectangles—more burlap flung by the villagers—appeared all over the face of the dragon and seemed to float down to the ground, creating billows of smoke.

"It's working!" Ben yelled, his high voice carrying above the commotion. "Keep going!"

He didn't need to tell Frank. Lydia's dad was already grabbing the next bag and running back to the fire. Lydia was bending over, her hands on her hips, panting, having just given the pump over to Jillisa, when she saw her dad run right where the fire had been just moments before. He flung another dripping bag at the thinning dragon. Lydia also saw what he couldn't see: fresh flames flying up behind Frank and swinging around him, like a mighty tail.

"Dad!" Lydia screamed.

He turned around, and through the flames Lydia could see terror on the face of the man who was never afraid.

She ran toward the fire, ready to plunge in after her dad and pull him out. But the heat was like a wall. She fell back, bawling. "Daddy!"

Suddenly, a mass of black rectangles covered the wall of flames, and Lydia's dad was running toward her, sweat dripping from his forehead. The villagers cheered and ran back for more burlap bags.

"I'm okay, Lydia," Frank said. "Let's keep fighting! We've nearly got it beat!"

He had soot all over his face and blood on his shoulder, and for a second Lydia wanted to beg him to stop, but he winked, and all her fear disappeared. God was with this dad of hers, just like he had been with Shadrach, Meshach, and Abednego in the fiery furnace, and she knew he would keep doing the right thing no matter what.

And she knew God was with him too.

The fire was dwindling, but so was the pile of burlap bags. "What else can we use?" Lydia yelled to Jillisa.

"De banana trees!" Jillisa yelled.

Lydia wasn't so sure that adding trees to a fire was such a good idea, but she and Ben ran after Jillisa anyway, leaving another girl to pump water.

"Where's Melvin?" Lydia called out as she ran. She couldn't remember when she last saw him, and she couldn't spot him now as she ran around the crowd of firefighters.

Jillisa didn't hear her. She led them to an orchard filled with funky-looking trees. The trunk looked like a giant leaf wrapped around itself, turned brown; huge green fanlike leaves opened up from the trunk right about the level of Lydia's head, and they seemed to her to be thrilled to break free of the trunk. Clusters of green bananas hung upside down right at the point where the leaves began.

"Here!" Jillisa yelled, grabbing hold of a huge swordlike thing. "Use these machetes to chop leaves." She handed each of them the tool and then picked up another for herself.

But it was slow going. Lydia's arms ached from holding them up, and the leaves were tough to cut through. Ben was doing alright, but Jillisa, who was quite a bit smaller than Lydia, hadn't made any progress.

"This is a good idea, Jillisa," Lydia called. And it was, because this many leaves would almost certainly smother the fire, "but we need some adults to cut them down. I'm going to get my dad."

"No!" Jillisa said. "We can do this!"

Lydia glanced back and saw that much of the schoolhouse had burned down and most of the fire was under control. But the part that was still burning wildly was reaching out and trying to lick the small house next to it. If that house caught fire, the domino effect might cause all the rest to catch fire too.

"We can do this," Jillisa said again, even more firmly.

Lydia whipped back to the tree and hacked as hard as she could. She whooped when a huge leaf fell down over her back, and she was banging on the next one before it even touched the ground. "We can do this!" she yelled.

They had just five fronds on the ground between the three of them when Frank showed up.

"What are you doing?" he yelled. He looked frantic.

"We're cutting leaves to put on the fire," Lydia said, handing the machete to him. "But I'm not very good at it."

Frank began hacking.

"It was Jillisa's idea," Lydia said.

Frank nodded. "Lydia, take the leaves to the water pump and tell some others to get over here."

"Come on," Lydia said to Jillisa. She grabbed the five fronds and went as fast as she could to the water pump. Jillisa followed. The burlap bags were all gone, but people were filling up buckets and pitchers and even cups. The adults who had come for water, covered in sweat and ashes, grabbed the banana leaves the girls had brought and ran back toward the fire. Others ran toward the banana trees.

Jillisa smiled just a little.

Lydia took over at the pump—the other girl was exhausted. But suddenly there was a giant swooshing noise, and the fire from the schoolhouse leapt onto the little house beside it.

When no one came to get water, Lydia, Jillisa, and the other girl ran to the banana field. Almost everyone from the village was there, either chopping or filling their arms with leaves. Lydia grabbed some leaves herself and followed the others toward the fire, which was eating up the little house and getting ready to latch onto the next one.

The invisible wall of heat was still there, but the fire wasn't as big as it had been, and they had a powerful weapon now.

"This way!" a large man called, leading all the leaf carriers to the part of the fire where the wind was at their backs. "All at once!" he shouted. "One! Two! Three! Throw!"

Lydia ran forward and threw the leaves as far as she could, closing her eyes. A wall of green went up against the wall of heat— and won. For an instant. And then a huge billow of smoke rose up and nearly swallowed her.

"Back!" the man yelled. "Back!"

The group moved back, and another group moved in. "All at once!" the man yelled again. "One! Two! Three! Throw!"

And another wall of green. And another billow of smoke.

But Lydia was already running back for more leaves.

"One! Two! Three! Throw!" She could hear the chant behind her as she grabbed more leaves. The field now looked like a random collection of warped fence posts with bananas on top, and she worried that they wouldn't have enough leaves.

"It be done!" someone yelled. "It be done!"

Lydia turned around and saw a mass of smoke, but no flames.

"Throw the rest of the leaves on just to be sure!" Frank called out, and everyone nearby did exactly as he said.

He ran back to Lydia and grabbed her tight. Ben ran up and got pulled into Frank's hug too. All the villagers were whooping and hugging and dancing, celebrating their victory against the fire, and Lydia could feel the adrenaline flowing through her own veins.

She was screaming out joyfully when Jillisa caught her arm. "Lydia," the girl cried, her eyes huge, "I can't find Melvin."

9
Missing

The celebration ended quickly. Lydia wondered why they had been celebrating at all—it was like cheering about saving a finger when your leg had been chopped off. The schoolhouse and one home had been burned down, the 4Runner was stolen, and now Melvin was missing.

"Everybody!" called the tall man who had been leading the fight against the fire. "Everybody come round!"

Lydia and Jillisa looked anxiously at each face that gathered in the darkness, but they could not find Melvin.

"Is everybody here?" the man called out. "Is everybody okay?"

"No!" Jillisa called out in a small voice. "My brother be missing!"

"And so," said Frank, "is Gretchen Hinkle."

Everyone was quiet for a moment, and then all heads turned toward the smoke that was still billowing up behind them.

"No," Frank said loudly, putting a hand on Jillisa's shoulder. "I don't think either of them are there. I saw them both outside about the time we started using the burlap bags."

"We search," the leader called out. He pointed to a few of the men, including Frank, and told them what sections of the village to cover. "De rest stay here," he said. He turned to Mrs. Young, "Your loss be greatest—your school and your home—so you lead us in song."

It seemed odd to Lydia that the one who was suffering most should be the one to sing. But when Mrs. Young began a sad song, and many of the others wrapped their arms around her and sang along, it looked comforting.

Jillisa and Sophia, though, stood back and looked ready to cry.

A very old woman hobbled over and squeezed Jillisa's cheek and patted Sophia's head. The old lady's smile showed that she had no teeth, and her words showed that she had no sense. "Melvin be a healthy baby," she said. "Very healthy."

Lydia and Ben stared, but Jillisa quickly explained. "She be my grandmother," she said. "She wonderin' what's really going on." Then she turned back to the old lady. "I know, Granny. He be okay." She put her hand on her grandmother's forehead. "Are you okay, Granny? You don' look so good."

"I be alright. But you don' be out here in de dark. When your father come home, we go to bed." The old woman pinched Jillisa's cheek again, took Sophia's hand, and ambled toward the singers, the young girl beside her.

Jillisa watched her go and then sat down on a stump and dropped her face in her arms. Lydia sat on the stump next to her and leaned forward, ready to listen. Ben stood beside them awkwardly.

"Melvin be gone," Jillisa whispered. "And now I got no one but Sophia."

"We'll find him," Lydia said. She just knew they would. He had to be someplace near.

"No, he be gone," Jillisa said louder. "Just like my parents and my sistah."

"I can imagine how you feel," Lydia began.

Jillisa stood up. "You got no idea how I feel! None of you! Our school be gone, our schoolteacher got no home, my brother gone . . ." She choked up for a moment, but then managed to go on. "And now you go your own way, back to your family and your television and your fat table."

"Jillisa," Lydia said. But the girl stormed away. Lydia watched her go, and then turned to Ben. "I feel awful!"

He nodded. "Do you think Mrs. Lynx did this?"

"I don't know. Just because we told some of her guests how bad things are for the Jamaicans? We didn't even mention the shark attack."

"Oh, yeah," he said. "How's your leg?"

"Actually, I forgot about it until now. I was too busy with other things. But it hurts now. And it's totally bleeding."

"I'll go get the first-aid kit," Ben said.

The first thing Lydia did when Ben came back was to swallow her painkiller. Then she carefully pulled off the bandage and began to clean the wound.

"I can sort of imagine how Jillisa feels," Ben said quietly as he watched her work.

Lydia glanced up at him.

He shrugged, looking a little embarrassed, and sat down on the stump Jillisa had left. "I was abandoned too."

"Yeah." Lydia wanted to hear more, but she didn't want to seem nosy.

"Yeah, my birth parents left me at an orphanage. My mom and dad adopted me when I was a year old."

Ben's pain didn't come out in anger or tears as Jillisa's had, but Lydia's heart hurt for him just as much.

"Wow." What else could she say? In a way she had been abandoned too when her own mother died in a plane crash eight years ago, but she hadn't been rejected or forgotten by her parents like Ben and Jillisa had. "I'm so sorry."

"I should talk to her," Ben said. They could see Jillisa sitting in a lawn chair behind the crowd. Some grownups were patting her head and squeezing her hand but Jillisa didn't seem to be comforted. She needed someone who understood.

"Yeah, I think that would be nice."

"Okay." He stood up and started to walk away.

"Ben!" Lydia said. "Please tell her that I may not understand, but I do care."

Ben nodded and went directly to Jillisa.

Lydia had managed to clean off all the blood from her leg and to pat it dry. She was just wrapping a new bandage around it when her dad walked up.

"How's the leg?" he asked.

"It was bleeding while I was running all over the place, but it's not bleeding anymore," she said.

"Does it hurt?"

"I just took a painkiller, so it should be okay soon."

"Oh, good. You've mastered that. When's the last time you took one?"

"An hour or so before bed."

"Okay. Just be sure to wait four to six hours before you take another one."

"I know."

Frank sat down on the stump and together they listened to the singing. It was beautiful. As they listened, Lydia watched Ben and Jillisa, who seemed to be deep in conversation. She was glad Jillisa was willing to talk to Ben, but she wished she could join them.

"You did a good job tonight," her dad said.

Lydia smiled. "So did you. We killed the dragon."

He laughed. "Yeah, that's what it was. Well, are you ready for another quest?"

"Another quest?"

"Yes." His face took on a serious expression. "I'm worried about Mrs. Hinkle and Melvin. I don't think they're here in the village, and I don't think they were hurt by the fire."

"Where are they, then?"

"I don't know," Frank said. "But we're going to find them."

Lydia didn't want to sit around and wait, not with Jillisa feeling all alone. She tried to think of what their next step would be. "Hink has a cell phone, doesn't she?" Lydia asked.

"Yes, but she's not picking up."

"Do you think the bad guys kidnapped them?" Lydia asked.

"I don't think they'd want hostages," Frank said. "And if they were kidnapped, you'd think we'd get a ransom note or something."

Lydia hesitated, and then said, "Do you think Mrs. Hinkle kidnapped Melvin?"

Frank stared at her. "Uh . . . no!"

Lydia blushed in the darkness. "It's just that she was acting kind of suspicious in Africa and—"

"No, Lydia. Mrs. Hinkle may be grumpy, but she's on our side. She's probably helping Melvin right now. They'll probably show up any minute."

Jillisa walked up with Ben, and Frank turned to them. "I think we should wait until morning before we do anything. If they're not back by then, we'll go to the Luxury Resort to ask questions."

Since their bedroom had driven off to who-knows-where, Frank pulled out a tarp and mosquito netting from his pack and borrowed blankets from the villagers. He created a comfortable place for the three of them to crash for the rest of the night—and crash they did.

Early the next morning Jillisa shook them from a deep sleep. Lydia looked at her watch. It was only seven o'clock.

"Come on!" Jillisa said, pulling on Lydia's foot. "It's morning. We have to go find Melvin now."

They had slept maybe three hours, but Jillisa probably hadn't slept at all.

"Alright," Frank said. "We'll pack up, get some breakfast, and then be on our way."

"I already made your breakfast," she said. "What do you need to pack?"

"We should take our tent here, the first-aid kit, and some food."

"How long will we be?" Lydia asked.

"It's about a nine-mile hike to the Luxury Resort," Frank said. "I doubt we'll make it there and back again in one day."

Lydia groaned and put a hand on her leg.

Frank looked concerned. "Maybe you should stay here."

"I'm going, Dad," Lydia said. "It doesn't even hurt." It didn't. At least not right then. It probably would once she started putting pressure on it. But she wasn't about to tell her dad that.

"You eat and get your things," Jillisa said. "I pack de food."

Thirty minutes later, the villagers stood silently as the foursome began their trek. Sophia was crying, but her grandmother held her tight.

"I be back, Sophia," Jillisa said. "I give your drawing to Marcy and bring Melvin home. I be back! I promise!" And for the next half hour Jillisa walked with a skip in her step, talking a mile a minute. "Now I get to see Marcy!" she said. "I hope Melvin not be having too much fun there without me."

Frank and Ben didn't say anything, and even Lydia was too tired to hold up much of a conversation. Her leg didn't hurt as much as she thought it would, and it wasn't bleeding, but this was a *long* walk. Among *lots* of hungry bugs. It was hard not to imagine how terrifying it would have been for Melvin and Hink to have walked through this jungle in the dead of night.

Even Jillisa's excitement wore off once they got past all the houses and followed the dirt road through the crop fields where many men and women were bent over working. She was no longer skipping or even smiling.

"Cheer up, gang," Frank said. "We've already walked two miles. Time to take a break."

Lydia looked at her watch. Sure enough; they'd been walking an hour already. Her leg was killing her. They sat on the side of the road and ate some of the bread, goat cheese, and papaya Jillisa had packed, and no one talked much.

"Can't we take a short nap, Dad?" Lydia asked.

"Do you think the Hobbits stopped to take a nap on their journey?" Frank asked as he began packing up.

"Yes!" Ben said. "They probably took second naps just like they took second breakfasts!"

"Ah, but on their quests they did not get second breakfasts, if you remember. They only wanted them."

Jillisa looked at the three Americans as though they had gone crazy.

"Oh! You've got to hear the story of *The Lord of the Rings!*" Frank said to her. And for the next hour, long after their break was over, Frank, Ben, and Lydia carried Jillisa through the trials and victories of the Middle Earth heroes. Sometimes, when there were no people nearby, they even reenacted scenes—Frank playing Aragorn, Ben playing Legolas, and Lydia playing Frodo. The walk was so much more fun, and everyone seemed to put the worries of this journey away.

Jillisa was a wonderful audience. She gasped and screamed and laughed at all the right places, and begged for more whenever the actors considered taking a break. "This all be in a book?" Jillisa asked during one of the breaks.

"Three books, actually," Ben said.

"I mean, someone made it all up and other people read it?"

"A man named J. R. R. Tolkien wrote it," Lydia said. "He drew maps of the imaginary world and even made up languages for it. And yeah, millions of people have read it."

"I did not know reading was for fun," Jillisa said. "I thought you only learn to read so you get a job."

"Oh, it's so much more than that," Frank said. "It's even more than having fun. Reading good books gets you thinking outside your own little world. It makes you much richer even if you don't ever get a job."

"I wan' read it," Jillisa said. "As soon as we find Melvin . . ." Her words faded out and a sad expression came on her face. "We will find him, right?"

Frank pulled the girl into a hug and kissed the top of her head, the same way he did to Lydia. Lydia grinned. "We're going to find him, Jilly," Frank said. "By the grace of God, we're going to find your brother. We're going to rebuild your school. We're going to bring in copies of all our favorite books for you to read. And you'll feel like the richest person on earth."

Jillisa smiled up at him with such joy and gratitude Lydia thought the girl might begin skipping again, despite the fact that her legs must feel like noodles by now. Lydia's sure did. With each step, the pain she had felt in her bad leg was replaced by numbness in both. "Dad, isn't it time to rest by now?"

Frank slowed down and looked around. Just ahead of them was a bridge over a wide river. "Man alive," Frank said. "I wish we didn't have to follow the road."

"We do have to follow the road," Lydia said.

"Following the river would cut our trip by a couple miles."

"Let's do it," Ben said.

Frank sighed. "It'd be fun, but we don't have the equipment for it."

"We've all got good shoes," Ben said. Jillisa had good sneakers, and the rest of them had hiking shoes.

"We'd need more than that. Right now it's a field beside the river, but up ahead you can see the jungle. We'd need machetes to cut our way through the underbrush."

"I don't want to hike through the jungle," Lydia said.

"Oh, you still have to, but we'll be on the road," Frank said. He stopped on the bridge and looked at the rushing water below. "Let's take a little break here and then move on."

"I keep going," Jillisa said. She was probably going crazy thinking about her brother.

"I can too," Ben said. But he plopped down on the ground as he said it. "Just give me a minute."

"In a minute you'll be sleeping," Frank said. "Sorry, Jilly. We've got to take a break."

Jillisa nodded.

Frank led them to the other side of the bridge, set down his pack, and sat in the grass beside the river. "Even with another break or two, we'll likely get there before lunch."

Great. If all went well, they'd make it through the jungle among screeching creatures only to show up at the shark-infested resort run by an evil witch. Lydia could hardly wait.

10
No Choice

The silence was spooky. The four travelers lay side-by-side in the grass beside the river, simply watching the clouds swirl above them. Lydia closed her eyes and tried to imagine that she was back home in her own yard—far away from Mrs. Lynx.

"Dad," Lydia said quietly into the silence over their heads, her eyes still closed.

"Mm-hmmm?"

"This is a Christian country, right?"

"Yes, many of the people on the island are strong believers in Jesus."

"Then how can God let someone as wicked as Mrs. Lynx get away with what she's doing?" Lydia asked. She felt Jillisa turn her head to look toward Frank. Lydia opened her eyes, but her dad kept his closed. Ben did too. Lydia turned her face skyward and shut her eyes again.

"If you mean attacking the village, we don't know for sure it was her," Frank said. "Though it likely was," he said under his breath.

"Well, at for making Jillisa's sister work so hard for so little. And not telling about the shark. And—"

"I get the idea," Frank said. "You're asking Job's question when he said, 'Why do the wicked live on, growing old and increasing in power?' And it's a question people have been asking ever since."

"Who be Job?" Jillisa asked. Lydia could feel Jillisa settle back in the grass, and she figured the girl was closing her eyes too.

"That's another story for you to read, Jilly," Frank said. "There is a book in the Bible about a man named Job. He was a good man, a righteous man. But Satan hated him. The Enemy told God that the only reason Job trusted God was because his life was good. So God allowed Satan to test Job. And the test was severe. Job lost everything—his home, his wealth, his children, his health. But he didn't lose faith."

"What be de answer to Job's question?" Jillisa asked. "About why God be letting de bad guys live on?"

"God didn't answer it directly. The Bible is full of promises that the wicked will perish, but it's also clear that God allows all people to make their own choices—and not everyone will choose as well as Job did."

"Choose?" Lydia murmured.

"Right. God is so good that he won't force anyone to do anything. He gives us opportunities all the time to choose good, even if we have chosen evil before."

They were quiet for a little while. A breeze blew over Lydia's face.

"I like God," Jillisa said.

Frank laughed. "Me too."

Lydia smiled, but was too tired to say anything else. She heard Ben's breathing grow slower. The breeze tickled her arms and the sun warmed her face. Lydia could hear the water running in the river and the birds calling out to each other in the sky.

She nearly gave in to the tug toward dreamland—but suddenly, water sprayed her face.

"Aaihh!" Lydia jumped up and yelled, wiping water from her eyes.

Frank, Ben, and Jillisa jumped up too.

"Wha—?" Frank hollered.

But Jillisa screamed for joy. "Melvin!" She bumped into Lydia as she raced for her brother.

Melvin stood at the edge of the river, getting ready to launch another water attack on the no-longer sleeping beauties, but quit when he saw Jillisa coming at him with enough force to knock him into the river completely. He held out his arms—whether to hug or to stop his running sister, Lydia did not know. But it wasn't enough. Both kids fell into the water, and came up splashing and spluttering and laughing.

"You be right, Mistah Barnes," Jillisa called out. "We found him!"

"What be talkin' about?" Melvin said, his arm draped over his sister's neck. "I found you!" And he promptly dunked her. Frank, Ben, and Lydia stood laughing on the shore.

Jillisa must have grabbed Melvin's legs, because a second later he got yanked under, and they both came up with Jillisa's arm around his neck.

"Yes, but you not be findin' us if we don' be lookin' for you," Jillisa said, and then she dunked Melvin. Quickly, she scurried out of the water, giggling, before he could catch hold of her. She stood dripping on the shore.

Melvin came out of the water himself and splattered the others.

"So what happened?" Frank asked. "Where have you been and where is Mrs. Hinkle?"

"Oh, mon," Melvin said, sitting down on the grass and wringing out his shirt. "Where do I start?"

Melvin had stood watching, horrified, as bits of the thatched roof of the schoolhouse fell down into the middle of the classroom and set the log benches on fire. But he couldn't stare long. He heard yells and saw Mr. Barnes get knocked down. And then suddenly that same man plus another were running directly toward him. Melvin didn't know what to do.

He spotted the open doors of the 4Runner and jumped in the backseat.

Wrong choice.

The men also headed for the vehicle and jumped in. They didn't seem to notice that Melvin was there, and he made himself as small as he could behind the passenger's seat.

"That dumb American, he left de keys in de ignition, mon!" the driver said as he started the truck up.

"What about de horses?" the second man said.

"Dey find de way back."

Melvin could feel the car spin around and he heard Ben yell to Mr. Barnes. "Watch out for that old lady!" the passenger yelled. Melvin dared to pop his head up for a moment, and looked directly into the eyes of Mrs. Hinkle. He instinctively reached out toward her, and she reached back—but the instant passed, and the car moved quickly out of the village into the darkness beyond.

They didn't go far, though. When the driver pulled over, Melvin could still smell smoke in the air. "What you doing, mon?" the passenger asked angrily.

"I want to watch," the driver said, getting out of the car.

"Watch?"

"Yeah, that's a big fire, mon."

"We get caught!"

"No, we don't. No problem. Dey think we long gone."

"Well, I'm not goin', mon."

Melvin felt butterflies in his stomach. He hated the driver for wanting to watch his village burn up, but he also needed the passenger to go or he wouldn't be able to escape.

"Hey!" the driver said from outside the car. "We got company!"

Melvin peeked out and saw Mrs. Hinkle coming down the road toward them, sitting on the back of a horse and holding the reins of another one.

"Hello, fellows," Mrs. Hinkle said. "Looks like you left your horses behind. Shall we make a trade?"

Both men were out of the car now and staring at her, their backs to him, and Melvin had to make a quick decision about what to do. If they gave her the car, he wanted to be in it. If they took her in the car with them, maybe he should try to save her;

after all, she was trying to save him. Melvin slipped over the backseat into the cargo area and pulled a blanket over himself.

"It's a fair trade," Mrs. Hinkle said. "You've made your escape and you can be well on your way before anyone comes looking for you."

"No, ma'am. We no can do that," the driver said. "But since you so kindly give youself to us, you come for a ride in the vehicle you ask about."

"Barney—," the passenger said, clearly about to protest.

Barney turned quickly toward his partner. "Don't you ever use my name in front of de hostage, mon!" Barney shouted. "And, yeah, mon, we take her. She see our faces, mon. Mrs. Lynx know what to do."

"So it *was* Mrs. Lynx!" Lydia shouted.

"Of course it was!" said Ben.

"And these were her hired men," Frank said. He whistled between his teeth.

"How did you escape, Mel?" Jillisa asked, as she stood with her arms and legs spread out in the sun, trying to dry off.

Mrs. Hinkle was pushed into the backseat of the car. As soon as Melvin dared, he reached around the seat to touch Mrs. Hinkle's shoulder. She squeezed his hand and didn't say a word.

"Where are you taking me?" Mrs. Hinkle asked.

"Wherever de boss say," Barney said.

"Which prob'ly mean Shark Bay," the other guy said.

Melvin heard a thud and Barney snarl, "Shuddup, Rupert!"

"Ouch!" Rupert said. "What did you do that for? And I thought you weren't supposed to say my name, mon."

"What do I care if she know your name?" Barney turned to Mrs. Hinkle. "You hear of Shark Bay?"

"Can't say I have," Mrs. Hinkle said. "Sounds like a delightful place."

"It's not," Barney said. "It be where Mrs. Lynx send de people who give her a hard time."

"Yeah, like her workers who want more money or time off," Rupert said.

"Shuddup!" Barney said again.

But Mrs. Hinkle said at the same time, "Wow. That's harsh. I hope you've never been sent there."

"No, not us," Rupert said. Melvin could imagine a big dopey grin on his face.

They were quiet for a moment and Mrs. Hinkle started humming quietly.

"My sistah's been to Shark Bay," Barney said quietly. Melvin almost didn't hear what he said.

"Your sister?" Mrs. Hinkle said.

"Yeah," Barney said. He cleared his throat. "You see? Mrs. Lynx be de wrong woman to mess with. We not botch dis job. So you let us do our jobs in peace."

Melvin could see Mrs. Hinkle reach forward and touch Barney's shoulder. "I don't think there is peace in this line of work, no matter how quiet I am," Mrs. Hinkle said. Melvin could hardly believe how brave she was. "But I can tell you how to find peace."

🐟 🐟 🐟

"That's the Hink I know," Frank said proudly. He looked knowingly at Lydia and then turned back to Melvin. "She preached them the Word, didn't she?"

"Yeah, mon," Melvin said. "Or at least she tried. It don't work. Dey made her shut up, and pretty soon we be at de Luxury Resort."

"You mean they pulled right up to the front door?"

"Yeah. I heard Mrs. Lynx yell at dem for that, and for taking prisoner, and for stealing de vehicle, and for leaving de horses."

"What happened then?"

"She told dem to bring de old lady to Shark Bay and hide de truck. Dey brought Mrs. Hinkle to a place just down de road from de resort. I not see much because it was dark, but dey had to go through de tiny little space between some rocks. I can show you!"

"But what happened to you?" Jillisa asked.

"I stayed in de car. Barney drove down de road and parked under some trees so people could not see it from the road. I stay until morning. I just started walking home about an hour ago. I had to get help. There was nothin' I could do for her all alone."

"You did the right thing, Melvin," Frank said. "I'm so glad you're okay."

"We have to save Mrs. Hinkle!" Ben said.

Lydia didn't like the sound of Shark Bay much, but she liked her own guilt over accusing Mrs. Hinkle even less. She knew they had no choice. Well, they did have a choice—and Lydia knew what they would choose.

11
Separate Paths

ink just better give me a good grade for this," Lydia said as she took a careful step forward on the road. Her leg was stiff and sore, but she didn't want to complain. With Melvin back plus new information to work with, they were motivated to continue their quest. Jillisa was literally singing and dancing. Even Melvin, who had filled his belly with food, was raring to go forward.

After just a couple minutes of walking, they had left the fields behind and were tromping through the jungle on the dirt road. The stiffness in Lydia's leg disappeared, and she even offered to trade her lighter pack for the heavier one.

"No, I'm fine," her dad said. "And in less than an hour we'll be back at the truck."

"And then what?" Lydia asked.

"Well, I'd like to avoid the Luxury Resort if we can. But it sounds like we have to walk right by it to get to Shark Bay. And I think Mrs. Lynx will be expecting us," Frank said. "She's got to know we'll be coming after Hink."

"I doubt it," Melvin said. "She not risk her own hide to save someone else, so she not be thinking anybody else do."

"I'm interested in this whole Shark Bay place," Frank said. "What do you suppose she does with her victims? Just shake them up a bit, I'm hoping."

No one answered, and they walked a bit faster.

"The good news is that I'm bound to lose weight from all this walking," Lydia said. She said it mostly to lighten up the mood of this grim party, but she also kind of meant it. The closer she got to the resort, the more she thought of the mounds of gourmet food people were eating—not to mention all the slim women on the beach who looked like they ate nothing but asparagus all day. She couldn't decide what she wanted more, the rich food or the slim body. But her comment didn't have the effect she was hoping for.

"Lose weight?" Jillisa asked.

"Yeah. You know, shed a few pounds." She squeezed her belly fat, which was really just a fold of skin, to show Jillisa what she meant.

But Jillisa looked at her strangely. "Why you wanna do that? You be weak if you lose pounds."

Ben grinned. "Can you see one of those anorexic supermodels on this hike, Lydia?" He made his legs look like wet noodles and he practically fell over as he pretended to try to walk on them.

The others laughed—even her dad—but Lydia felt stupid.

"What be anorexic supermodel?" Jillisa asked, still laughing at Ben's goofy behavior.

"Oh," Ben said. "In America girls think they have to be half dead to be beautiful."

"Half dead?"

"Yeah, skinny. They starve themselves."

Jillisa burst out laughing. "That's de stupidest ting I ever heard. Do you be telling fibs?"

"No fibs," Frank said.

"And people really think dey look good?" Melvin asked.

That made Frank laugh.

Not Lydia, though. All three of the other kids were now doing the "waif walk," as Ben called it, and Lydia wanted to sulk for a few hours—but then Jillisa fell.

At first Lydia thought she did it on purpose. Jillisa almost floated down and sank onto the road. She sat there looking up with a surprised expression on her face.

"Is everything okay, Miss Jilly?" Frank asked.

"Umm . . . I don't think so," Jillisa said.

"What de problem?" Melvin asked. "Your ankle be bad again?"

Jillisa's eyes filled with tears and she nodded. "I be so sorry."

"You don't need to be sorry for anything," Frank said. "What happened to your ankle?"

"When I be little, I twisted it," Jillisa said. "It been all swollen and hurting. It took long time to get better. Now it be twisting all de time. I shouldn't be walkin' like that."

"It's not your fault," Frank said.

"Can you walk?" Melvin asked.

Jillisa tried to stand up, but she couldn't put any weight on her left ankle. "Oh, no!" she cried. "What am I going to do?"

"Maybe I can carry you on my back," Melvin said.

"She's as big as you are, Melvin," Frank said. "I'll be the one carrying her. Good thing you've almost dried off." He winked at her and then turned back to Melvin. "I really hope you can find that 4Runner, though."

"No problem, mon."

"Do you have the keys?" Ben asked.

Frank shrugged. "I don't need keys." He took off his pack and pulled out the tent. "I'll have to come back for this later." He shoved it under a bush and turned to Melvin. "Now the pack is just the right weight for you, Melvin." He turned and grinned at Jillisa, who was still sitting on the ground. "And I'm free to give you a ride now, Miss Jilly." He knelt down in front of her with his back welcoming her. "All customers aboard, please."

They hadn't gone much farther when they saw the main road ahead.

"Hey!" Melvin started running toward the road. "I think I hear a car coming! Maybe we hitch a ride."

Lydia could hear it too, but she didn't have enough energy to run. Her wounded leg wasn't killing her, but it wasn't fun to run on.

"Hold up," Frank said. "They're going east; we need to go west."

Melvin stopped and stared at the road ahead. Suddenly their own 4Runner went coasting by.

"Hey!" Frank said, running right past Melvin with Jillisa still clinging to his back. The car hadn't been going fast, but by the time they got to the main road a moment later, it was gone.

Ben ran to catch up to Frank. "Did they have Mrs. Hinkle with them?"

"I didn't see," Frank said.

Melvin and Lydia caught up, and they all scurried onto the main road, which was still quite remote and empty. Frank squatted down and touched a trail of oil on the ground. "The car is leaking oil," he said, "which means this little trail will lead me right to them."

"Hansel and Gretel," Lydia said. She didn't have time to explain, but she would have loved to get Jillisa hooked on all the old fairy tales too. Oh! Jillisa had a world of books waiting for her.

"Let's go," Frank said, heading down the road after the car, Jillisa jiggling on his back like a rag doll.

"But Shark Bay be that way," Melvin said. "Mrs. Hinkle might still be dere."

It was like being at a potluck dinner and trying to decide what food to put on your plate. Only it wasn't like that. Lydia had to get food off the brain. This was not a potluck—it was possibly a matter of life or death.

"Melvin, you know the way to Shark Bay, right?" Frank asked.

"Yes."

"And I'm the only one with a driver's license," Frank said.

The others all nodded, waiting.

"Jilly has to come with me," Frank said, bouncing her. "So that leaves the two of you." He turned his eyes on Ben and Lydia.

"Shark Bay, sir!" Ben said, putting his hand up to his head as if he were in the military.

Lydia grinned and pulled herself to attention too. "Shark Bay, sir!" she said.

Frank sighed. "Your job is reconnaissance only, you hear?"

"Recona-what?" Melvin asked.

Frank smiled. "Scouting. Watching. Collecting information so that we can strategize our next move. Now, hopefully I'll get that truck back and be over there to help you soon." He got directions from Melvin to Shark Bay, told Lydia to turn her phone on because she should be getting service pretty soon, and then turned right.

"Bye, Mel!" Jillisa called. "You be careful!"

Perhaps "be careful" meant not strolling through the front door of the Luxury Resort. But after walking another hour and a half, they were tired, and they all needed water. Besides, Melvin had never seen the place before, and he was excited to see his older sister.

They stepped into the lavish foyer, Melvin's eyes nearly popping out of his head. It was lunchtime, and vacationers were everywhere. Lydia could see them at the pool to the right of the foyer and at the restaurant to the back. She supposed many were on the beach and some were playing tennis or racquetball. The lobby, however, was wide open, and the hosts at the front desk barely glanced at them, probably assuming they were already guests. Lydia spotted the soft couches and couldn't resist making a beeline for them.

Just before she sank into the nearest couch, a silky voice from beside them said, "Ah, it's Lydia Barnes and company. We were expecting you."

Lydia was too tired to fight or run. The only energy she could conjure up bought her about one whole second to sit on the couch, which was even softer than she remembered it. She felt no fear as the tall black man with no front teeth approached her, just annoyance. All she wanted was to curl up on the couch for a nap. After that, he could take her off to fight sharks all day if he wanted to.

"Ms. Barnes," the silky voice said as a rough arm pulled Lydia to her feet.

Lydia looked up at Mrs. Lynx, and was almost surprised to discover that the woman she had been hating for the last two days was still quite beautiful.

"I see you could not resist the allure of this place," said Mrs. Lynx, running her manicured fingers over the couch. She smiled, looking as proud as Lydia had felt winning the spelling bee last year. She looked at Ben now. "Did you have enough of the jungle?"

Ben and Lydia both looked up at Mrs. Lynx with their jaws clenched. Melvin stared at the floor, and Mrs. Lynx acted as though he didn't exist.

"Where is your father, Lydia?" Mrs. Lynx asked.

Lydia shrugged.

"You don't know?" the woman asked. She paused dramatically. "Well, don't worry. I know." She put her hand on Lydia's arm as if the two were best of friends. "I'm afraid he's gotten himself into a bit of trouble, but I'll see what I can do to help him out."

Lydia wasn't sure if Mrs. Lynx was lying, but she could still feel her belly getting hot.

"And your sister is well taken care of too," Mrs. Lynx said to Melvin, looking at him for the first time. When he jerked his head up, with terror written all over his face, Mrs. Lynx laughed. "She's got such an awful sprain. Shame. She might have made a wonderful maid."

94

Melvin couldn't take it anymore. His eyes burned with hatred. "You'd better—!"

Mrs. Lynx looked as disgusted as she would have if a used diaper had been flung at her. "Stop!" she cried, showing more ruffled feathers in that one word than Lydia had seen before, but the woman quickly composed herself. "Please do not bring such . . . unpleasantness onto my premises." She turned to the man who now stood threateningly behind the kids. "Let's not keep our tired guests standing here. Would you please show them to their room?"

The man laughed, then herded the kids out the door of the lobby.

12
Luxury Revisited

Much to Lydia's surprise, she and the boys were not escorted directly to Shark Bay without passing go or collecting $200. They were brought to a room—smaller than the one she had before, but still quite luxurious. It had a bathroom and two double beds, complete with a television and warmed, fluffy yellow towels.

The guard winked at Lydia when she looked at him. "You be a regular guest here," he said. "Eat all you want, mon. Have fun. But don't think about stepping a toe off de resort."

Lydia figured, from what Melvin had told them earlier, that this guy was Barney. Besides being tall and having no front teeth, he was overweight. He wore a red muscle shirt and basketball shorts with Nike sandals.

"Where is my dad?" Lydia asked.

"And my sistah?" Melvin asked.

"And Mrs. Hinkle?" Ben asked.

The man only laughed and shut the door.

Lydia ripped off her backpack and threw it into a corner of the room, and the guys quickly did the same. She yanked her cell phone out of her pocket and nearly screamed when she saw that she had service. She dialed her dad first then Hink. Neither picked up. "Where are they?"

"Call the police," Ben said.

Lydia just shook her head. "They've got that covered." She pointed to a phone in the room. "Do you think they would have left a phone for us if it would help us at all?"

"We got to find dem. Jilly can't even walk!" Melvin said, sounding as though he were ready to cry.

"I'll call Cynthia," Lydia said, and Ben nodded.

"Who?" Melvin asked.

Ben explained as Lydia dialed. Cynthia was a sixty-something-year-old black woman who was boss to both Ben and Lydia's parents—and one of Lydia's favorite people in the world. Cynthia didn't have Mrs. Lynx's stunning cheekbones or slim waist, but she had a regal manner that made her entirely beautiful, for real.

"Lydia!" Cynthia's cheerful voice filled Lydia's ear. "You must have sensed me. I'm just one island over from you."

This was good news! "You're in Cuba?"

"No, I'm in Haiti, directly east of you. We can just about wave to each other." Cynthia laughed. "I wish we could see each other, Lydia. I miss you, girl."

The kindness in Cynthia's voice almost made Lydia start crying on the spot, but she simply didn't have time for that luxury. She needed to save her dad, not cry about him. Lydia sank down onto one of the beds and told the whole story. Ben flopped onto a large overstuffed chair, and Melvin curled up on the other bed.

If Lydia had called any other adult, she would have been told that everything was going to be alright, that the authorities had everything under control, that Mrs. Lynx was clearly showing great kindness by keeping them there while her dad . . . *was being fed to sharks!*

Cynthia, though, didn't lead Lydia to a mental breakdown like that. She listened carefully and asked important questions like "What time was it when you last saw your dad?" "Where exactly were you?" "What does Jillisa look like?"—and then told Lydia to stay close to her phone. "I'm going to get to the bottom of this."

The guys had already fallen asleep. Lydia took a long hot shower, her phone right outside the tub. She was careful not to get soap in her wound, but really she wasn't too worried about her leg. It wasn't as swollen as before and wasn't bleeding at all. She had even forgotten to take her pain meds for awhile.

Thankful for the bathroom luxuries—although, surprisingly, no longer thrilled about them—Lydia rewrapped her leg, dried her hair, and changed into clean clothes. She washed the clothes she had been wearing in the bathtub and then hung them up to dry.

Lydia checked her phone for service—three bars—and then put it in her pocket. "Come on," she said to the guys, shaking Ben's foot. "Let's go eat."

Ben slowly raised his head and then reluctantly agreed. Melvin, though, was dead to the world. They couldn't even get him to quit snoring.

"He hasn't really slept since the fire," Lydia said.

"Let's just leave him a note and bring something back for him," Ben said.

"Uh . . . he can't read," Lydia said.

"Oh, yeah. Well, let's just go quick. We'll be back before he wakes up."

Lydia didn't know what else to do. "Okay, let's go."

The buffet was still open, and it was exactly the same as but totally different than the last time Lydia ate there. All the foods were beautifully displayed and promised to be gloriously delicious, but this time everything looked odd—like a parka in the desert, or a giraffe in a car, or a prom dress at a funeral. It was just too much.

Lydia took a few of the small tuna fish sandwiches, a big bowl of tomato soup, and a few scoops of chopped fruit. And then she made up the same plate for Melvin, adding some french fries to his.

They started walking back to their rooms with their food, relieved they hadn't bumped into Mrs. Lynx, when Lydia found herself staring straight into the face of Tom Adams, the British man who had taken the horseback tour through the village.

"You!" Tom said. "You're Frank Barnes's daughter." He smiled so big that Lydia could see a piece of strawberry stuck on one of his molars. "So you folks are back then, are you?"

"Just for a little while," Lydia said, not sure how much to tell. "Hey!" she said, having a sudden brainstorm, "did you ever get to telling people around here about the village?"

Tom looked over Lydia's shoulder and said, "Not much. I mean, I did collect a few magazines from folks to pass on to the school, but I'm still working on the other stuff. Excuse me. I have to go." And off he rushed.

"Magazines?" Lydia said as she and Ben walked on.

"Well, maybe there will be some fashion magazines, and we can show Jillisa the anorexic models," Ben said, laughing.

But Lydia was mad. Tom hadn't kept his word. "Or maybe there will be one on home and garden," she said bitterly. "That would be useful to the villagers. I'm sure they're all wanting to learn how to decorate their homes for Valentine's Day."

Ben was still cracking up. "Or one on body building. Because, like, they have so many gyms around here."

"Or on weight loss. Maybe they can learn to eat fresh food." The sarcasm didn't make her feel any better.

"Still," Ben said, "it's not such a bad idea to try to gather up reading material from folks. Especially now. The villagers have lost everything."

Lydia wished she could round up copies of the *Learn-to-Read Bible* and give one for each of the kids at the school. She nodded. "Maybe we could even get people to donate paper and pens and stuff. Just whatever they have that they don't need to take home with them."

Lydia was getting excited now, and walked faster. She wanted to get lunch out of the way so she could start asking around for help. She had to do something while she waited for Cynthia to find her dad.

But when she turned the corner on the walkway toward their room, she saw their door swinging open. "Melvin!" she said. She managed to balance both plates as she stormed into the room, but she would have preferred to see tomato soup smeared all over the floor to what she saw now. "Melvin!" she called weakly again. But the small room revealed no secrets. Melvin was gone.

13
Hoodlums

There's no sign of a struggle," Ben said. "Melvin could just be out trying to find lunch."

"We would have seen him," Lydia said. "And why would he leave the door open? Come on, we have to go ask Mrs. Lynx."

"Mrs. Lynx?"

"We're not going to lose another person, Ben!" Lydia said.

"I know!" Ben said. "But she won't tell us anything. We have to look for clues."

"This is not a treasure hunt!" Lydia said. Back when she had been in Liberia with Ben, they had uncovered a mother lode of treasure by deciphering clues. "Or even my own stupid reputation!" In Israel, Ben had helped her—via e-mail—to figure out who had framed her as a thief and a vandal. "This is someone's life!" And to think Lydia had once thought this would be the easiest trip of them all.

"We can find him, Lydia."

"Maybe we can just wander around the entire resort until we realize he's not here!" Lydia said.

"Sarcasm is not cool, Lyd," Ben said.

She scowled. "Well, let's get started then."

They set their plates down and walked out the still-open door. They turned left, away from the direction they had been coming from before, because if Melvin had been going that way, they would have seen him. They had to squeeze around a housekeeper's cart—and then Lydia heard Melvin's voice. Only he wasn't speaking slowly like he usually did. And he was happy.

"Melvin?"

Melvin called out, "Yeah?"

"What—?"

But Lydia stopped herself from what surely would not have been a pretty display of emotions—a whole mix of relief and joy and anger—when the assistant manager of the resort stuck her head out the door.

"Ms. Young!" Lydia said.

"It is you!" the woman said at the same time.

Lydia took a breath, ready to begin explaining themselves, when Melvin stuck his head out the door too.

"There you be at last," he said. "This be my sistah."

"Marcy?"

The young woman nodded and put her arm around her brother, smiling as though she had just won an Olympic event. "Thank you for bringing my brother to me. A gift from God! I don' often clean de rooms, but an employee was sick, and I was covering for her. What a surprise to find Melvin sleeping in de room I was cleaning!"

Lydia laughed, picturing the scene. "We just brought lunch to the room. Do you want to eat with us?"

Marcy shook her head. "No, I must work. I must not accept gifts from guests."

"We're not guests!" Ben said. "We're prisoners. Didn't Melvin tell you?"

"I began to," Melvin said. "Marcy—"

"Wait," Marcy said. "I don' stand here talking. I get caught. I go to your room."

Once in the room, Melvin spotted the food immediately. When Lydia showed him which plate was his, he tore into it. Lydia then told the whole story to Marcy—since Melvin's mouth was full—and handed Melvin her plate when he had finished his own food.

"So where be Jilly?" Marcy asked.

"That's what we're saying!" Ben said. "We don't know where any of them are."

"My dad's boss is looking into it," Lydia said. "But meanwhile we're stuck here."

"Do you have any more food?" Melvin asked.

"There's plenty," Lydia said. "But we've got work to do. We can eat later."

Finding Tom Adams wasn't very difficult. His big belly was easy to spot on the beach, where he lay lounging on a chair, soaking up the rays.

"Hey, kids," he said when they walked up, but he didn't move a muscle. The woman he was with did, though. She got up and walked away. Lydia shrugged and sat sideways in the empty chair with each boy on either side of her.

"We need to talk," Lydia said.

Tom took off his sunglasses but didn't sit up. "What's up?"

"We love your idea of collecting reading material from folks to give to the school," Lydia said. "But we want more than magazines."

"We want books and paper and markers and pencils," Ben said.

Melvin didn't say anything, but that's who Tom looked at. "Would that help?"

"Yessah," Melvin said.

"Do you know how to read?"

Melvin looked down. "A little bit, sah."

"Do you want to learn how to read?"

Melvin's head popped up. "Yes! I do!"

Tom finally sat up. "Well, then, I'll give you every book I have here. And every pen. And every piece of paper. Where should I bring it?"

Lydia hadn't thought of that. She hesitated for a moment, but Ben spoke up. "We'll have a box right outside room 109. Tell your friends."

"I shall!" Tom said, smiling a little. "Do you need it now?"

"The sooner the better," Lydia said. "And if you don't do it now, you might forget later." She sounded like her dad.

Ben elbowed her and glared as if to say, "Don't be rude!" But Lydia just shrugged. What she said was true. And this was too important to worry about whether she was hurting someone's feelings.

"Sounds good," Tom said. He stood up and walked away. "Save my seat, won't you?"

"Ummm. . . ." Lydia wanted to say no so she could start talking to other people about donating books, but that would be *unnecessarily* rude. "Okay," she said. "But please hurry."

They didn't have to wait long. An American kid wearing bright orange surfer shorts walked up a moment later. "Hey, aren't you the people who started that water fight?" he asked. "I thought you guys left."

"We're back," Lydia said. "But I'm not stepping foot in the water again."

"Why not?"

Lydia remembered her dad telling Mrs. Lynx he would say only the truth—and then promptly being escorted off the premises. She had two causes to fight for here, and her time could be short. "I got attacked by a shark. That's why we left."

"Nuh-uh," the boy said.

"Uh-huh!" Ben said. "Show him, Lyd."

Lydia pulled the bandage off and showed the thirty-seven stitches to him. "My dad knocked the shark with his elbow, which must have stunned it enough for me to get away."

"For real?"

"Yes, for real. My dad says it must be a rogue shark that the Marine Police should relocate."

More and more people gathered around to hear the story and to see the wound. Lydia knew she had to use all this attention wisely. "You know what, though," she said. "Instead of swimming, you can help us gather school supplies for a village not far away. It's Melvin's village."

Melvin smiled and said, "All de cool people be doing it, mon."

Everyone laughed, and before Tom came back, Lydia had already convinced six other people to donate. Ben had run off to find a box, and Melvin sat there smiling and answering people's questions. And it wasn't just kids surrounding them anymore.

Everyone was very interested in talking to Melvin and finding out how the fire got started at the village.

Lydia didn't come right out and say Mrs. Lynx did it—she wasn't that dumb. But she did tell them the school had been burned down on purpose, the villagers were devastated, and her dad was investigating the situation.

"Well, why don't we all go over there for an afternoon? With the lot of us working, we should be able to get a new structure in place straightaway," Tom said. He turned to the crowd. "It's not too far, and since none of us are foolish enough to swim with that rogue shark about—"

"Yeah," the first kid said. "It'll be fun!"

"How does tomorrow work?" Tom asked, and many in the crowd nodded.

Lydia was excited. Her dad would be so proud of her—once Cynthia found him—but Melvin shook his head. "I don' know if that's a good idea," he said. "You spend time at my village, you will find it hard to come back here. It be very, umm . . . *much* here. You be feeling embarrassed, mon."

"The boy is right about one thing," that infamous silky voice said from behind the crowd. "It's not a good idea." The crowd parted and Mrs. Lynx, wearing tan slacks and a glittery black halter top, sauntered to the front of the crowd. She stood behind Melvin and put both hands on his shoulders in that maddeningly matronly way. "Going out to that village would be very dangerous for you," she said, looking in the eye of each person with great *fake* compassion, "and I'm just talking about the diseases. As we state in all our literature, leaving the resort should be done only under the protection of our guides, who can help you to discern whether a need is real or"—and here she smiled at Melvin as if he were her favorite grandchild—"fabricated."

Melvin had probably never heard the word *fabricated* before, but he must have figured out what it meant. "We not be making this up!"

"They ask for books, which are items of great value here," Mrs. Lynx began.

And, of course, Ben chose that moment to come running back, yelling, "I've got a huge box! Lots of room for all your stuff!"

The crowd opened and Ben stopped short when he saw Mrs. Lynx.

"Items of great value," Mrs. Lynx continued, turning away from Ben and looking at each in the crowd again, "that they cannot use. They admitted it themselves: They have no school."

"It got burned down last night!" Lydia said.

"So they say," Mrs. Lynx said, still with that horrid expression on her face that made people think she adored children.

"I was there!" Lydia said. "I helped put the fire out!"

"Just like you were attacked by a shark?" Mrs. Lynx asked sweetly, reaching out to touch Lydia's shoulder.

"She *was* attacked by a shark!" Ben said. "You know that."

Mrs. Lynx looked at him as if he were a bright bouquet of flowers. Then she turned back to the crowd. "Folks, don't let these kids trouble you. I'm so sorry for letting them interfere with your vacation." She sighed deeply and changed her expression to one of complete sorrow. "I shouldn't have let them here at all, but I couldn't resist helping children in need. This little girl's father"—she touched Lydia's shoulder again—"was just imprisoned for dealings with drugs."

Lydia jumped up, her face burning. "He was not! You—"

"Where is he then, Lydia?" Mrs. Lynx asked softly.

Lydia almost cried. "I don't know!"

"And I," Mrs. Lynx said louder as she pressed down on Lydia's shoulder with surprising strength, "am keeping Miss Lydia and her companions safe until other accommodations can be made for them. Please, folks," Mrs. Lynx said to the crowd quickly, since Ben and Melvin were starting to argue now, "go back to your vacations. Let me take care of this."

The people looked from Mrs. Lynx to the kids, clearly not knowing whom to believe. Lydia put her face in her hands and cried. She just couldn't bear to watch them all walk away, not when they had been so close.

"Come on, children," Mrs. Lynx said.

When Lydia raised her head she saw Barney and another guy, probably Rupert. This guy was only a bit taller than Lydia and bounced back and forth from one foot to the other—fidgeting worse than her best friend Amy without her ADHD medicine. He wore glasses and a do-rag.

"Where are we going?" Lydia asked, feeling like a bug on its back.

"I've got a perfect spot for you," Mrs. Lynx said. "Someplace where you won't be a bother to my patrons."

"Where?" Ben demanded.

Mrs. Lynx smiled brightly and looked each of the children in the eyes before answering. "You're going to a lovely little place called Shark Bay."

Lydia didn't expect Shark Bay to be pretty. But after she was forced down a narrow rock staircase and past a metal gate into the dreaded prison, she had to catch her breath. It was gorgeous. They stood at the back of a cove. The rock floor went all the way to either side of the twenty-acre enclosure and up to the white sand that spread for about three hundred yards toward the blue-green water. In the middle of the rock floor, straight in front of them, was a magnificent old building that was covered in wild plants—an abandoned castle or resort. They could look directly through it to the other side, where the ocean went as far as they could see. The sun shone high in the afternoon sky, making the sand shine, the water sparkle, and the castle glow.

"Welcome to Shark Bay, mon," said Barney, yanking the gate shut behind them. "I be right at de top of de steps, so don' be tryin' anyting funny."

The three kids stood staring at their surroundings, saying nothing.

Finally Ben made a low whistle. "Wow," he said quietly. "If things were different, I'd pay good money to explore this place." Yeah. If Lydia's dad wasn't in jail and their teacher and Melvin's sister missing. And if they weren't prisoners.

"I think this is the other side of that cliff we walked to, Ben," Lydia said. "And it was probably Barney on top of the hill."

Ben nodded.

"We got to get out of here, mon," Melvin said. "We got to find Jillisa."

Lydia pulled her cell phone out of her pocket. No reception. "Let's see if Hink and Jilly are here."

Melvin began walking toward the building, calling "Jilly!"

"Mrs. Hinkle!" Ben called.

"Jillisa! Hink!" Lydia called.

"They're not here," Ben said. "Let's see if we can find a way out of this place."

"Shouldn't we check inside first?" Lydia asked.

"In there?" Ben asked.

It did look a bit creepy now that they were up close to it. It wasn't nearly as big as the building at the Luxury Resort, but this one was several stories high. The windows above them were dark, and the birds even seemed to avoid flying near the openings. The rock it was built from was old and covered in some sort of ivy, making it look forbidding.

But if Hink had to spend the night in this cove, she probably stayed inside. Lydia went first. She walked up the marble steps covered in ivy and moved toward the huge doorway. Much like the Luxury Resort, this building had no doors or windows, just wide spaces meant to let in the light and warmth.

"Jilly?" Melvin called, walking in behind Lydia.

Lydia smelled the campfire before she saw it. Even though there were no doors or windows in the place, indoors wasn't exactly the best place to build a fire. And when Lydia walked around the corner into the main lobby, she saw coals smoldering on the floor right by the fireplace. Not in the fireplace, but beside it. And between the fireplace and the campfire was a pile of blankets and a nearly empty jug of water.

"Hink?" Lydia said.

Nothing but the scurrying feet of mice could be heard.

"Let's see if we can find her," Ben said.

"Better still—a way out of dis cove," Melvin said.

"Okay," Lydia said. "But shouldn't we make sure this fire doesn't go out? In case she's gone?"

"We not be needing it," Melvin said. "We be getting out of dis place."

Lydia wasn't so sure. "Just in case."

Ben walked to the corner of the room where some driftwood and dead branches had been piled. He threw some on the fire and then blew on it. It caught, and the small campfire crackled happily. "There. Now let's go check things out."

"Shouldn't we try to find something to eat first?" Lydia was hungry. It was nearly two o'clock, and Melvin had eaten her lunch a couple hours ago.

Melvin glared at her and then walked over to the water jug. "Here."

Lydia opened it, sniffed it, and then took a big swig. It wasn't exactly cold, but it still did the job. Lydia handed it to Ben, who also chugged some down. After Melvin took his share, the jug was nearly empty. Lydia set it back down and then pulled the blankets back.

"What are you doing?" Ben asked.

"Looking for this." Lydia held up a football-sized package wrapped in brown paper. She opened it, and found a loaf of bread and some cheese. "I don't know where she got it, but Hink must have put it here so the mice wouldn't find it." Lydia quickly divided the food between the three of them and they all ate. "I wonder where she is now? We should go look for her."

Ben rolled his eyes at her, but started walking toward the doorway.

"Let's go that way," Melvin said, pointing to the other side of the resort toward the back door.

"Okay."

The main floor was fairly open, and had marble floors and marble pillars and a marble staircase. Lydia could imagine cleaning the place up, lighting the giant chandeliers above them, and creating an elegant ballroom. The guys, though, didn't allow her to look around much. They rushed through to the other side where they had a perfect view of the ocean.

They also had a perfect view of the creatures this resort was named after.

14
Shark Bay

hy de sharks be doin' that?" Melvin sounded completely amazed. "De sharks be acting strange, mon!"

Ben and Melvin ran toward the shore to get a better look, but Lydia hung back.

"Come on, Lyd," Ben called. "They can't get you out of the water."

Lydia wasn't so sure. "Melvin said they're strange," she said. "Who knows what they could do?"

Ben laughed. Things were as bad as they could possibly be, and Ben laughed. "Sharks don't have feet, Lyd," he said, practically snorting through his nose as he expressed his glee over her fear.

Even Melvin chuckled. "For somebody so brave, you sure be scared."

Lydia groaned and walked toward the beach. She was sure her leg throbbed more with each step, as if the shark who had taken a piece out of her could sense her approaching.

Once she got there, though, she had to admit it was a pretty cool sight. The sharks swam around in circles, crowding each other without bumping into each other. Sometimes they would put their eyes above water and swim toward shore and Lydia could see the water sliding into their mouths, past the jagged, crooked, numerous teeth.

"Well," Ben said after a few minutes, "we're not going to escape by water. Let's look around to see if we can climb the cliff."

They walked around the entire cove and found a dark cave with a very small entry that they couldn't get themselves to enter without a flashlight. Their sweet host had neglected to give them their backpacks. The cliff had a terrible overhang that made the climb impossible—except in one spot.

"It's impossible!" Lydia said after attempting to climb for several minutes without ever getting both feet off the ground. The rock wall jutted straight up and was as smooth as glass.

"Look!" Ben said. "Hink must have been here!" They could see a handprint of blood on the wall that had to be fairly recent. It was brown already, no longer red, but it would clearly wash away the next time it rained.

"It looks like she cut it there," Lydia said. They saw one lone foothold just out of their reach; it had a splotch of blood on it too. "She got higher than we did."

"That's not bad, mon," Melvin said, impressed. "For an old lady."

"You don't know Hink," Lydia said. "I wonder if she escaped."

They all looked up to the top of the cliff to catch glimpses of the jungle beyond. "No way," Ben said. "Not even Hink could climb this."

"What next?" Ben said.

"We could check out the cave," Lydia suggested.

"You crazy, mon?" Melvin yelped.

"For someone who is so brave, you sure are scared," Lydia said, smiling a bit.

Melvin grinned back, and they walked slowly over to the cave and stood looking at it.

"So, you think there will be an exit on the other side?" Ben asked skeptically.

"I don't know," Lydia said. "But it's worth a try. We have to get out of here somehow."

"Don't you think Mrs. Lynx's men would have checked it out themselves before they kept prisoners here?" Melvin asked.

"Probably," Lydia said. "But not for sure. Come on." She stuck her head in the entrance of the cave. It reeked. Worse than the cave in Bethlehem her friend Mitri had shown her. She pulled her head out again.

"What did you see?" Ben asked.

"I didn't see anything," Lydia said. "I only smelled." Then she took a deep breath and stuck her head back in, and her shoulders, and her feet. She could stand up straight, and when she reached up, she couldn't feel a ceiling. She put her hand on the smooth cold wall and began walking around the cave, keeping her eye on the entrance. She saw Ben come in, and then Melvin.

"This way," Lydia said. "Keep your hand on the wall."

But at that very moment, the ceiling came crashing down on top of her.

Lydia screamed and grabbed her head. The stuff falling on her head was coming quickly, and she thought for sure she would be buried alive.

"Bats!" Ben hollered. "Get out!"

Lydia almost felt relieved for a moment, and then realized she didn't want to die by having her blood sucked either. And she couldn't see the door.

She looked around desperately and saw the bright spot for an instant, and then it disappeared again. She ran straight for it, her arms still over her hair. She could hear the beat of the bats' wings and feel them rubbing against her. The light showed up again, and Lydia was almost there. She dove through the doorway, scraping her bad leg on the rock. Ben and Melvin were running away from the cave toward the building.

"Wait for me!" she called.

They didn't. And Lydia's leg was hurting again. The bats were still streaming out of the cave, but they were all flying up and away—not toward Lydia at all. "Oh," she said out loud. "I guess my blood's not good enough for them."

She walked into the resort, where Melvin and Ben were leaning up against a wall and breathing heavily. "Thanks, guys," she said. "You're real heroes."

The boys looked guilty for a moment, and then Ben said, "So you didn't find an escape route then?"

Lydia punched his arm lightly.

"Ouch!" Ben said, but he was grinning.

"Let's take a break," Lydia said. They must have been exploring for a couple hours already, with no luck. "Let's go sit on the back steps."

They walked to the back of the house and were surprised to see Barney and Rupert both at the shore. Barney was dumping a large barrel full of garbage into the water, what looked like food scraps. Rupert was throwing rocks at the sharks that were yanking the floating debris down as soon as the waves delivered it to them.

"This be our chance!" Melvin hissed. "De gate be open."

"Back through the house," Ben said. "Come on."

The three of them slipped unnoticed back into the building and ran quickly through it. This time Lydia didn't stop to admire the ballroom or to worry about the pain in her leg. They stopped at the front entrance and glanced toward the ocean where both men were now throwing rocks.

"Go for it!" Ben whispered.

Together all three kids ran toward the open gate without once looking back. Melvin got there first, then Ben, and then Lydia, who was still limping a bit. They ran up the steps—straight into a tall Jamaican man with a gun. His skin was chocolate and his eyes were hazel, and Lydia was surprised by how good-looking he was. Only he was bad-looking too. Kind of like Mrs. Lynx.

"Sorry, children," the man said, waving the gun in their direction, "but no one escapes from Shark Bay." He nodded once toward the steps, and the kids quickly ran back down—stopping at the other side of the gate. The man followed them down and slammed the gate shut. He locked it and said through the bars in a quiet, menacing voice, "Don' try anything like that again."

Lydia heard the venom in his voice and nodded; then she turned toward the yells of Barney and Rupert. They were running toward the gate, shaking their fists. "Hey, mon!" they yelled. "Open it!"

Lydia, Ben, and Melvin didn't move, and the wicked man on the other side of the gate stood there smirking at them until Barney and Rupert arrived, completely out of breath. "I thought you might mess this up," he said. "Good thing I stuck around after hauling de trash."

Barney grabbed hold of the gate and shook it. "Open up, Fred."

Fred smirked again, and then pulled out his keys and unlocked the gate. "Don' be stupid even one more time," he told them as they walked through. "Or I feed you to de fishies." He prodded them each once with the gun, smiling, and then walked up the steps and out of sight.

Barney turned around and looked at the kids. "What you lookin' at?"

They were staring at their escape route, which had been ripped away from them.

"Yeah!" Rupert said. "You pull a stunt like that again and you get us killed!"

The kids walked slowly back to the building. "That's not such a bad idea," Ben said quietly.

Lydia and Ben sat down on the front steps, but Melvin walked in circles. "Let's do it," he said.

"What? Kill them?" Lydia asked. She didn't even look up from the circle she was drawing in the sand with her toes, revealing the unforgiving rock below.

"Yes," Melvin said.

That got both Ben and Lydia to look up right away. "Are you kidding?" Ben said. "Even if we wanted to, we couldn't take them on."

"Look," Melvin said, pointing to some tree branches hanging over the cliff far above their heads.

Lydia couldn't see anything special.

"Ackee fruit," Melvin explained. "If we can knock some down, we can poison them."

Ben and Lydia just stared at him.

"Listen," Melvin said, looking desperate. "We must get out of here. We must help Jilly."

Lydia imagined how stressed out Jillisa must be, whether she was being held captive or set free to try to make it home alone on that bad ankle—with no idea where her brother was. Then Lydia thought of her dad. She didn't know if he really was in prison or if he was tied up in Mrs. Lynx's personal torture chamber, but either way, he needed help. There was no way Mrs. Lynx would have set him free. He could do too much damage. Plus there was Mrs. Hinkle. Who wasn't so evil after all.

Lydia looked at Ben. "We do have to get out of here."

Ben nodded.

Melvin walked toward the overhanging branches. The other two followed. "We be needing rocks to knock them down."

"And then what?" Ben asked.

Melvin lifted his hands and scrunched up his face to show that he didn't know.

Lydia was nervous. "Maybe we can just threaten them with it."

"How?" Ben asked. "Say, 'If you don't let us go, we'll make you eat poison seeds'?"

"This is dumb." Lydia turned back to the steps. "It won't work. And I don't want to kill anyone."

The boys followed, and everybody sat back down again.

A few minutes passed and then Ben blurted, "I don't want to kill anyone either, Lydia." He sounded embarrassed.

Lydia looked at him, and then shoved him a little. "I know you don't."

"Well, I don' either, mon," Melvin said. "But I do want to get outta here."

Lydia looked up at the sky to see where the sun was. They had just a few more hours before nightfall. "I don't think that's going to happen tonight."

"I think you're right," Ben said. He stood up and headed inside. "I'm going to make sure the fire is still going."

"Good idea." Lydia stood up and walked out toward the beach. "I'm going to make a sandcastle."

"What?" both boys asked.

"Nothing else to do," Lydia said. "We can't escape. And I'm not going to sit here sulking."

After about ten minutes, Melvin and Ben quit moping by the back steps and joined Lydia.

The sun was hanging over the coast, a burnt-orange ball that scattered orange light through the sky and over the water. Things looked pretty bad, but that sunset rolled on down as beautiful as ever. God was still there.

Their sandcastle was gorgeous, and Lydia was glad they had chosen to quit stressing out and just to leave themselves in God's hands. Still, God wouldn't want them to be stupid. "Let's set up camp," she said.

Setting up camp amounted to making sure the fire was going and distributing the blankets evenly. But with the darkness settling in around them, no one wanted to go back outside. Within an hour, Melvin was sound asleep.

Not Lydia. It was one thing to sleep inside a 4x4 truck with metal doors in the jungle. It was another to sleep in the pitch-black night on the floor of a doorless building in the middle of nowhere with only a dying fire and two scrawny boys for protection. Lydia's stomach growled, and the ground seemed to get harder every time she flipped into a new position.

"Ben?" she whispered. "Melvin?"

Neither of them answered, and Lydia felt a pang of jealousy that they could sleep so easily. Then she remembered that Melvin had had to sleep all alone last night. Of course, knowing that someone is worse off than you doesn't actually make your situation better. Lydia was still hungry and tired and uncomfortable—only now she felt bad for complaining about her own pitiful problems.

Lydia managed to drift off to sleep—and woke to the sound of scuffling near the doorway to the room they were sleeping in.

15

SOS

ydia sat up. The fire had nearly gone out and early dawn was creeping into the room. "What was that?" Neither Ben nor Melvin answered. They were sleeping so soundly that they looked as if they were enjoying a feather bed at the most luxurious resort.

The scuffling continued, and Lydia could feel the back of her neck prickling.

"Who's there?" she whispered into the darkness.

Uh-uh-uh-uh-uh-uh-uh. Whatever was making that noise was not human. It sounded like a squeaky door closing, or maybe a dolphin with a cold—which made her start thinking about sharks. On shore. Coming to get her.

"Go away!" she yelled. She threw a stone toward the doorway and heard the clatter on the marble floor. But the squeaking and scuffling continued.

Lydia was about to get up to find a stick or something, when suddenly the noise stopped and silence settled back over the building.

"What's going on?" Ben asked.

Melvin raised his head too.

Lydia felt her face get hot even though there was no way they could have known she was imagining four-legged sharks.

"Something was out there," Lydia said. "Let's go check it out."

It was easy to recognize the markings of a snake on the dusty floor. "A snake!" Ben said. "It could have wandered up and had us for breakfast."

To Lydia, that sounded better than being shark bait.

"Nah," Melvin said. "There be no poisonous snakes here, mon. It be just a common snake."

"Still." Ben shuddered.

"Look," Melvin said. He pointed to the ground where the snake trail was now one straight line surrounded by little footprints. "A mongoose got it."

"A mongoose? Isn't that a little squirrel?" Lydia asked.

"What be a squirrel?" Melvin asked.

Ben laughed. "A squirrel and a mongoose look a little bit alike, but the mongoose is bigger—and it has sharper teeth."

"And it attacks snakes," Lydia said.

"What does the squirrel eat?" Melvin asked. "Fruit?"

"Sometimes," Ben said. "But usually nuts."

"Well, I'm glad it didn't get us," Lydia said. "And all this talk about fruit and nuts is making me hungry. What can we eat around here?"

"Nothing," Melvin said. "Unless you want to go fishing."

They walked back to the fire and Ben threw some more driftwood on to keep it going, and then they walked to the back door to sit on the steps, overlooking the ocean.

"What do we have to work with?" Ben asked.

"What do you mean?" Lydia asked.

"Well, clearly there is no way to escape this island with our bare hands. If we had a boat or a ladder, we could get out."

"Uh, we don't have a boat or a ladder," Lydia said.

"I know," Ben said, clearly annoyed. "But we do have other resources. We just have to think of them."

"We have dem trees," Melvin said. "We can make a ladder."

"Maybe," Ben said. "We don't have nails or rope, though."

"We have those blankets," Lydia said. "We could make a rope."

"Good thinking."

"Or we could use it as a trampoline and fling someone up." Lydia smirked.

Both boys stared at her, but, kindly, neither of them said, "Stupid thinking."

"We have brains," Ben said after a moment. Lydia's lack of use of them must have triggered that thought for him.

Melvin snorted, but Ben continued. "Seriously. We know where we are—"

Lydia nodded. She had studied the map of Jamaica and knew that they were on the western tip of the island.

"—and we know people will be looking for us."

Lydia nodded again. Even if her dad was in jail and unable to save them, Cynthia wouldn't leave this alone.

"I not be waiting around for that," Melvin mumbled.

"We can read and write," Ben continued, listing the "resources" on his fingers.

"How do that help?" Melvin said.

Lydia remembered that Melvin couldn't read very well yet, and wondered if Ben had hurt his feelings. Ben was about as clueless as her dad when it came to thinking about people's feelings.

"We could make an SOS message on the beach," Ben said.

"SOS?" Melvin asked.

"Yeah, it's a distress signal," Ben said. He stood up and began walking toward the beach.

"It means Save Our Souls," Lydia said. She followed Ben.

"No, it doesn't," Ben said. "That's just what people made up later. It started off as Morse code." He glanced over at Melvin, who was walking with them. "Morse code is a bunch of dots and dashes that represent letters. People used to use it to send messages to each other through telegraphs." Another look at Melvin showed he understood nothing of what Ben was saying. "Whatever," Ben said. "It doesn't matter. What's important now is that we get the letters SOS onto the beach somehow. As big as possible."

"Why?"

"In case an airplane comes by," Lydia said. "If someone sees it, they'll know to send help."

"Nobody here know that code, mon," Melvin said.

"Pilots will know it," Ben said. "It's an international code."

"If you say so." Melvin shrugged and then looked around. "We could use branches from the trees."

Lydia was relieved the discussion had not turned into a fight. Melvin seemed pretty stressed out. She wondered if he had ever been apart from his sister before. "How will we cut them down?" Lydia asked.

"We'll just have to look for dead branches," Ben said.

The kids went straight to work, and Lydia tried to ignore the rumbling in her belly. Ben and Melvin collected the branches because Ben thought a snake might drop into Lydia's hair. Sometimes the guys had to climb into the trees to crack off a dying limb, and Lydia thought for sure one of them would fall and break his neck. Meanwhile, Lydia dragged the branches to the middle of the beach and formed the letters so they were even taller than she was. Every time she caught a snatch of the boys' conversation, it was about Morse code. Apparently Melvin wasn't as offended as she thought he was. He didn't know how to read, but he was clearly smart.

It took only a half hour to finish the job, but all three kids were sweating by the time they were done. And the sun was just barely peeking over the cliff behind them.

"Now what?" Melvin asked.

"Let's go for a dip to cool off," Ben said.

He started walking toward the water, and Lydia screamed.

Ben turned around, laughing. "I'm only messing with you."

Lydia socked him in the shoulder, and Ben shoved back.

"Hey!" Lydia said. Then she grinned. "You're asking for it, pal!" She put both hands on his shoulders and tried to shove him to the ground.

Ben laughed and pushed back.

"Get him, Lydia!" Melvin yelled.

Lydia had just got Ben to his knees and was about to make him eat sand when she heard that horrible, silky voice behind her. "Not very ladylike, in my opinion."

Ben and Lydia jumped up and Melvin turned sharply around.

Mrs. Lynx, more beautiful than ever in silk cargo pants, a white top, and white heels, stood smiling before them.

And next to her stood Jillisa.

16
No Lie

J illy!" Melvin ran to his sister and hugged her so hard Lydia thought he would squeeze the tears out of her. Jillisa didn't cry, though. She laughed and hopped around on one foot, kissing her brother on the back of his head as he held her.

Lydia tore her eyes away from her friends and glanced up at the gate to see if it was open.

"No, Ms. Barnes," Mrs. Lynx said, laying a hand on Lydia's shoulder. "It's not time to leave yet."

"Where's my dad?" Lydia said. She took a step away from the woman whose beauty now seemed repulsive to Lydia. This woman was like a stunning flower blossom that smells like vomit.

"He's still in prison, my dear." Mrs. Lynx somehow managed to pull an expression that looked utterly believable in its pity. "I'm so sorry."

But Lydia didn't fall for it. "When are you going to let us out of here?"

"Soon. I wish I could let you come back to the resort, but after what happened yesterday . . ."

Ben stepped up. "Where's Mrs. Hinkle?"

"Mrs. Hinkle, dear?" Mrs. Lynx asked, looking at Ben as if he had just materialized out of nowhere. "I have no idea."

"You know exactly where she is!" Melvin said. He had an arm around Jillisa's waist, and she leaned on him, keeping her left foot off the ground. "I—"

Lydia was sure that he was about to blurt out that he had been in the car—and Lydia knew that would be bad information to give this wicked lady. The last thing she needed to know was that Melvin was a witness. "We need food!" Lydia said. "Keeping us here without—"

"Yes, yes, of course," Mrs. Lynx said. "Finally someone here is being reasonable and thinking about their own problems rather than everyone else's. Of course you need food. And I've brought you some." She led them up toward the resort, talking to the kids as if they were adoring students.

Lydia wished she could stay right where she was just so Mrs. Lynx wouldn't always get her way, but Lydia needed that food too much. Jillisa hopped along beside Melvin, and Lydia could see the tracks in the sand that the girl had made on her way down to the beach—one-footed. Plus Mrs. Lynx's spiky prints. Poor Jillisa must have had to lean on the vile Mrs. Lynx on the way down. There is nothing worse than having to get help from the very person who is tormenting you. It would be like asking the teacher who failed you to explain the math problem.

"I would have brought you food last night," Mrs. Lynx said, "but I was busy working with the authorities, trying to get your father out of prison." She smiled lovingly at Lydia. "I knew you'd consider that to be of utmost importance."

Lydia didn't believe her for a second, but she still wanted to know what was happening. "When is he getting out?"

Mrs. Lynx shook her head, looking at Lydia as sadly as if a puppy had been hit by a car—or, in Mrs. Lynx's case, as if a guest had not signed up for another trip to the resort. "It's not looking good," the woman said. "It's not only drug charges he's facing. Apparently he set fire to a school out in the back-country. That's a serious crime. We who have been here for so many years working with the Jamaican people are so aware of what a problem illiteracy is. I'm sure if your father had known—"

"Stop!" Lydia screamed. They were back at the front door of the resort, and the guards were inside the gate watching the whole scene. They stepped forward when Lydia freaked out, but Mrs. Lynx held up a hand.

"My dad did *not* start that fire and he did not have drugs. My dad is the one who—"

"Ah, Lydia," Mrs. Lynx said quietly, trying to shush her.

Lydia didn't shush. "—helped create that school and who fought to put the fire out and who cares about the Jamaican people so much more than you do. *You* are the one—"

"I need you to stop now," Mrs. Lynx said.

Lydia was surprised at the power of Mrs. Lynx's voice, which was fairly quiet. She stopped.

"I understand that you are in deep pain and confusion, but I cannot allow you to lash out at me."

She paused and stared at Lydia with such concern and strength, that Lydia wondered if the woman believed her own words. There was no one here to fool, and yet Mrs. Lynx was carrying on as if the entire police force were watching.

"It is clear," Mrs. Lynx said, "that I cannot bring you back to the resort yet. The guards will give you your food as soon as you destroy the SOS code." She turned and headed toward the gate, her hair swinging behind her like a television commercial for Head and Shoulders.

"Wait!" Ben said.

Mrs. Lynx turned.

"When are we going to get out of here?"

"I'm hoping to get you on a flight back to the States this evening."

"What about us?" Melvin said, his arm around Jillisa.

"Once your friends are gone, you will be free to go," Mrs. Lynx said. She turned back to the gate, spoke to the guards in low tones, and disappeared up the steps without a backward glance.

"What happened, Jilly?" Melvin asked the moment they were alone. "Are you okay?"

"It was terrible!" Jillisa shuddered and sat down on the step. "Dey caught us soon after you left."

"Hey, kids!" yelled Barney from the other side of the gate. "Go get dose sticks or we'll eat de food ourselves!"

"Tell us in a minute," Ben said to Jillisa. "You wait here, and we'll pull those branches into a pile. Maybe we can make a bonfire to attract some attention after we eat."

"Good thinking," Lydia said.

Jillisa stayed where she was, and the other three ran down to the beach. They pulled all the branches into a pile in less than five minutes, and then ran up to the gate. A large barrel sat just inside the gate. Barney must have put it there when they were gone. Now he sat on the other side of the gate on the bottom step.

"Good stuff," Barney said, and the kids started reaching in to pull out food. He had a large Danish in his fingers, and red jelly dripped down the side of his mouth. "Mrs. Lynx, she treat you right, mon. A private resort with room service." He cracked up at his own joke, showing the space between his teeth.

It was hard work moving the wooden barrel all the way to the building. It was big enough to fit two large beach balls in it, but there was definitely more than air packed in this baby. Lydia could hardly wait to get it to the patio so they could dump it out and see what the booty was. Her mouth was watering just from looking at the pineapple and oranges on top. She half expected to find rocks under the fruit, but even the food she could see was better than nothing.

Mrs. Lynx surprised her again. The barrel was full of fruit and bread and pastries and cold chicken and jugs of water. And all of it was delicious. And fresh.

"So, what happened, Jillisa?" Melvin asked as he yanked a piece of fried chicken off the bone.

Shortly after the two groups had separated, Frank and Jillisa caught up to the 4Runner. It had broken down, and sweat was dripping into Barney's eyes as he watched Rupert's feet sticking out from under the car. Mrs. Hinkle's beady eyes were poking out from the backseat.

Frank pretended not to see Mrs. Hinkle. He set Jillisa down and walked up behind the men. "Need any help?"

"Who are you?" Barney asked.

"I'm Frank." He stuck out a hand. Jillisa could hardly believe he was telling the truth. He should have made up some story. Lydia wasn't surprised to hear it, though. Her dad never lied, even to save his own skin. "I'm a little off course, here," Frank said after they shook hands. "But I know a thing or two about cars. If I get your car going again, will you drop me off at the Bayside Hotel?"

"You got a deal, mon," Barney said.

Frank went to work on the car while Barney and Rupert sat back in the shade, watching him work. Once in awhile they picked up their cell phones for brief, quiet conversations, but mostly they kept to themselves. Frank ignored Mrs. Hinkle, besides nodding his head at her politely once. He might have done that to any stranger. Jillisa sat at the side of the road, waiting to see how this would play out.

Frank discovered that the oil they had seen on the road was dripping from the loose oil filter. Frank was able to tighten it with his hands, and he knew there was a spare quart of oil in the back of the SUV. Good thing Barney and Rupert were busy on their cell phone.

After about fifteen minutes, he had the problem solved. As soon as the car was fixed, Barney gestured to the backseat. "Hop in, buddy."

Once they were in the car, with Jillisa squished between the two Americans, Frank introduced himself to Mrs. Hinkle. She smiled, looking as sharp as ever. "Where you headed?" Frank asked Barney as soon as they pulled onto the road.

"Negril," Barney replied.

"Great!" Frank said. "That's exactly where I'm going."

Barney turned around and grinned. "That's right, Miser Barnes."

Frank looked up sharply.

"You and your lady friend here be going to de police station." Rupert laughed. "Good thing you fix de car or we never make it."

Frank sat back in the seat for a moment, and then he surprised Jillisa by laughing. "Well, you sure got me!" he said. He turned to Mrs. Hinkle and gave her hand a squeeze—a proper hello—and then turned back to Barney. "How did you figure out it was me?"

"Not too many white folk 'round here, Franky," Barney said. "Plus de boss knew right away when we tell her 'bout you."

"Yeah, Mrs. Lynx is pretty clever," Frank said.

"She think she is," Rupert said—and Barney shoved him. "What?" Rupert said. "He knows it be her already."

Frank just smiled. "So, what are we going to jail for?"

"Drug possession and arson," Barney said, grinning.

"So, Mrs. Hinkle and I set that school on fire, did we?" Frank said, nodding his head.

"You sure did."

"And where did we get the drugs?"

"No idea," Barney said with a grin. "But de cops will find dem right here in de glove box."

"What about the girl?" Frank asked. "She's got a sister at the Luxury Resort. You could just drop her off there. That act of kindness might get you some sympathy from the judge when you're arrested for this."

Barney turned around sharply.

"Yeah," Frank said. "This little scheme isn't going to work. And it will be your necks on the guillotine, not Mrs. Lynx's. But it's your call."

"You think—?" Rupert said.

"Shuddup!" yelled Barney.

"Your dad musta scared him," Jillisa said. "Because Barney, he brung me to Ms. Lynx, and den Rupert, he left with your dad and Mrs. Hinkle. Mrs. Lynx kept me in one of de hotel rooms until she brung me here. But what happened to you?"

After the whole story was told and half of the food was eaten, Lydia picked up a paper bag holding about six chocolate-covered donuts. She stood up and marched toward the gate.

"What are you doing?" Ben asked.

"I'm going to ask Barney to let us go."

Ben jumped up. "Why? You'd have better luck asking the sharks to let us go."

Lydia turned around. "That's not true. You can't talk to sharks."

"You can't talk to those guys," said Jillisa.

"Maybe, maybe not," Lydia said. "But humans can at least choose good or evil. Sharks can't. It's possible that Barney and Rupert will do the right thing."

All three kids looked at Lydia as if she were crazy, but Lydia walked up to the gate anyway. "Umm, Barney? Sir?"

He was sitting at the top of the steps now, but he came down right away, looking surprised. "What you be doin'?"

Lydia held the paper bag through the bars. "I just wanted to give you some more donuts. We've had enough to eat."

He looked at the donuts the same way her dad looked at apples in Halloween baskets, as if they were poisoned or something. "What you tryin' to do?"

"I'm just hoping that if we're nice to you, you'll let us go," Lydia said. If the truth was good enough for her dad, it was good enough for her.

Barney put his chin up in the air and laughed. "You be crazy, just like you dad." But he grabbed the bag and then crammed a donut in his mouth.

"How is my dad?" Lydia asked.

"Oh, he be fine, jus' fine." Barney laughed again and Lydia got a lovely view of the contents of his mouth.

"What do you mean?"

"De jail not be as nice as de resort here."

Lydia looked around. "It isn't bad in here, actually."

Barney looked at her as she had just said that slugs are pretty. "How's de swimming?"

Lydia shuddered. "I already got attacked by a shark once. I'm not going for that again."

Barney glanced quickly at her. "That shark bite be for real?"

Lydia remembered that he had been in the room when she was getting her stitches. "Of course it was."

"What it be like?"

Lydia sat down cross-legged on the rock floor and told the story, trying her best to sound as dramatic as her dad always did when he told people about his escapades. "That shark was nothing compared to the rebel soldier I faced in Africa," Lydia said.

"Soldier?" Barney sat on the bottom step. "I got to hear dis."

Lydia grinned and told the story about her adventure in Africa. After fifteen minutes of watching Barney squirm, she said, "I wish you had been there, Barney. Ben and I could have used your help."

Barney's chest swelled and he shook his head. "I wouldn't do nothing crazy as that."

Lydia beckoned for Ben to come up, and the other kids did too. They each sat down on the rock floor, making a semicircle around the gate. "Ben, I was just telling Barney about Big Henry."

Ben nodded.

"So, you live out there in Africa?" Barney asked.

Ben nodded again.

"Why? You don't look like no African to me." He laughed. Lydia wondered if the reason he laughed at his own jokes was because no one else did.

"My dad's a doctor and likes helping the people who can't afford care," Ben said.

Barney shook his head. "All you people crazy," he said. "What a job!"

"What about your job?" Lydia asked. "Do you like it?"

Barney stared at her. "Don't jive me, mon. I got to feed my family too, you know."

"I was just asking," Lydia said. "Still, aren't there any better jobs than holding little kids captive and putting innocent men in jail?"

"Nuh-uh," he said. "I don' know how to read, how to write. Here in Jamaica, dis be a good job."

"So, if you could read, you'd get a better job?"

Barney glared at her, but Lydia just smiled, her hands folded in her cross-legged lap.

"Maybe," he said.

"Well, then I'll teach you to read."

He stood up quickly, as if he had seen a spider crawling on him.

"I've met your boss," Lydia said, not moving, "and I sure wouldn't want to work for her. Maybe if I can teach you to read, you'll be able to do something else."

"I be de enemy, kid," he said, waving his arms around wildly. "You see dis fence? You be in jail."

"Like I said, maybe if I'm nice to you, you'll change your mind."

"I won't."

Lydia shrugged, feeling perfectly calm. She was actually kind of having fun. "Oh, well. At least it will give us something to do while we wait for Mrs. Lynx to decide what to do with us. I'm a good teacher, you know."

He shook his head. "You might run away."

Lydia held his gaze. "We won't escape. We promise." She looked at the others. "Don't we, guys?"

Ben and Jillisa nodded, but Melvin looked at Lydia like she had gone insane. He turned away, his feet pointing toward the ocean.

Lydia touched his shoulder. "Come on, Melvin. If we escape, then Barney gets in trouble. We can't do that to him."

Melvin obviously didn't see a problem with that. But he shrugged and stood up. "Don't matter. We not get away."

That seemed good enough for Barney. He pulled his keys out of his pocket and opened the gate, while Lydia, Ben, and Jillisa scrambled to their feet.

"We'll have to go down to the beach so I can write in the sand," Lydia said.

Barney looked at her suspiciously, locked the gate, and followed her toward the water.

Lydia turned to Ben. "I think we should start with the alphabet," she said. "What do you think?"

"That makes sense," Ben said.

Jillisa, leaning on her brother beside them, said, "But I already know de alphabet."

"Hey, mon," Barney cut in, "she be my teacher, not yours."

"Ben," Lydia said quickly, "why don't you work with Jillisa and Melvin. I'll work with Barney."

"What should I do?" Ben said. "We don't have any books."

"Have them spell out words. Start with easy words, and keep pushing them to get harder ones. Have them memorize spelling words."

"Okay," Ben said. He didn't look confident.

"Thank you, Ben!" Jillisa said. "I want to read better. I want to read books about Frodo!"

"Everyone find a stick," Lydia said. "You'll need that to write in the sand." They all reached into the pile of branches they had planned to use as their escape route, then the three other kids went farther down the beach and Lydia scratched the alphabet in large letters right where she and Barney were.

Barney caught on quickly. He easily copied the letters and happily sang the famous little ditty to memorize them. When Lydia laughed at him for singing out of tune, he tossed sand at her, grinning like a little kid. The tougher part came when he tried to remember what sound each letter made, especially the vowels, but Lydia patiently coached him.

An hour sped quickly by.

"How you learn to read, mon?" Barney asked. "You just a kid."

"My mom taught me." Lydia didn't remember a lot about her mom, but she did remember crawling in her mother's lap every night and listening to Winnie the Pooh stories. Her dad recently told Lydia that her four-year-old self thought she could read a chapter book before she even knew her alphabet simply because she had the book memorized. Lydia smiled.

Barney looked down. "She be worried about you, don' she? And your dad."

Lydia shook her head. She sat down in the sand and looked at the water. It looked so green and beautiful. It was hard to believe danger lay just below the surface. "My mom died when I was six."

Barney sat down beside her, but he didn't say anything for a little while.

Jillisa and Melvin were sitting in the sand looking toward the ocean, but totally focused on Ben. Ben was standing in front of them talking about something, and his hands gestured wildly. A gust of wind blew up from the water and tossed sand in Lydia's face.

"Sorry, mon," Barney said.

Lydia shrugged. "Don't worry; be happy, right?"

"Nah, mon. Life be hard, even for rich American kids."

Lydia missed her dad. He was the one who must be worried about her. "I wish I could talk to my dad," she said.

Barney shook his head. "He be in jail."

He drew a circle in the sand, and ran his finger around and around it so that it dug deeper to the dark, wet sand. "I get you outta here," he said after the circle had started to fill in with light, dry sand.

Lydia looked at him. What was he talking about?

"She never let you go," he said.

"Yes, she will," Lydia said. "She'd get in too much trouble if she didn't."

"She not be getting caught."

"Oh, she will. And she knows it. We have friends and family back home who will come looking for us. Actually, they already are."

Barney looked quickly at her. "What you mean?"

"I called my dad's boss when we were at the Luxury Resort."

"How you do that?"

Lydia pulled out her cell phone.

"Oh."

"You're the one who has to get out of here," Lydia said. "You don't want to stay mixed up with Mrs. Lynx. She's bad news."

Barney stood up. "Come on, kids!" he yelled to the others. "We getting out of here!" He took huge steps through the sand toward the gate, and Lydia had to run to keep up. The others were close behind. "Rebel soldier Big Henry change his mind. I change mine too."

"Mrs. Lynx will kill you!"

"Den hurry up. She be back soon."

But by the time Barney had unlocked the gate, Mrs. Lynx was there, smiling on the other side.

17

Parting Company

Going someplace, Barney?" Mrs. Lynx asked.

Barney glanced at Lydia, and then smirked. "Just checkin' things out, ma'am," Barney said. He pressed on the gate, but Mrs. Lynx had it firmly closed with her foot. "De kids clean de beach like you say. But dey messin' 'round again, and I go see what dey up to."

"Well, at least you locked the gate behind you this time. What was going on?"

"Dey playin' school, ma'am."

Mrs. Lynx laughed but didn't move her foot.

"Ummm," Barney said, "has de plan changed?"

"Why should it have changed, Barney?"

"Well, we got a problem."

"What's that?"

"De girl"—Barney pointed at Lydia with his thumb—"have a cell phone, and she call someone."

Mrs. Lynx's eyes got big. For once she looked slightly surprised.

Lydia probably looked even more surprised. What was Barney doing? She wasn't sure if Barney had gone back to the dark side or not, but she kept her mouth shut. She was going to have to take her chances with him.

"And why hadn't you taken it away from her?" Mrs. Lynx asked.

"I not see it, ma'am."

"Well, look closer next time." Mrs. Lynx looked at Lydia. "Who did you call, sweetie?"

"My dad's boss," Lydia said, holding her head up high. "She's taking care of the situation as we speak. My dad will be out of jail before the day is over. I suggest that you start packing your bags before she gets here with the police." Lydia was bluffing a little, but she really didn't doubt her own words. Cynthia would come through for them.

Mrs. Lynx smiled. "You are a sweet child," she said coldly. Then she stepped away from the gate and stood at the bottom of the steps looking up, one hand on her hip. Barney finished unlocking the gate and went through without looking at the kids.

"Leave it open, Barney," Mrs. Lynx said. "The plan has not changed. It is now time to part company with these lovely children."

"You're letting us go?" Lydia asked.

"Whatever do you mean, Miss Lydia?" Mrs. Lynx said, turning around to face her again. "You make it sound as if you were held captive." She nodded to Barney, who held the gate open.

Lydia stared at the woman as she walked through the gate. Either this woman was delusional or she thought Lydia was the biggest moron on earth. Of course they were being held captive. And something weird was going on now.

"You're going home," Mrs. Lynx said once all the kids had passed through the gate and stood at the bottom of the steps.

"What about my dad?" Lydia asked.

"And Mrs. Hinkle," Ben added.

"I'm afraid they will need to stay in the country a bit longer," Mrs. Lynx said. Then she ushered them up the steps. "But come, your ride is waiting."

"I'm not going home without my dad," Lydia said, not budging.

Mrs. Lynx laughed as if Lydia had just made a charming joke. "I'm afraid you don't have a choice, my dear," she said as she went up the stairs. "You are now in the hands of authorities outside of my control."

"What do you mean?" Everyone else was going up, so Lydia did too.

"Child protective services. Clearly your dad is unable to take charge of you."

"You can't—"

Mrs. Lynx spoke over her, smiling as if there had been no interruption and everyone was hanging on her every word. "Ben, of course, will be going back to his own parents, who are very concerned about him right now, and quite angry at your father, I'm afraid."

They got to the top of the stairs and all of Lydia's protests were cut off.

"Marcy!" Jillisa and Melvin both screamed.

Their older sister was standing next to Rupert outside the 4Runner. "Jillisa!" Marcy called back. "Melvin!"

Mrs. Lynx turned to Melvin and his sisters. "You children are currently trespassing. If you do not leave immediately, I will have to press charges."

The twins glanced at Lydia and she made her eyes really big and nodded toward the road. "Go!" she mouthed. They all started moving at once, with Jillisa hopping.

"Wait," Mrs. Lynx said. The kids turned. "With all due respect, I do not wish to see any of you again. You have simply caused too much trouble." She looked as though she deeply regretted not being able to see the angels again. "I have to ask you to please not come near my resort again. I would be heartbroken if you forced me to take action to ensure this."

"Come on," Marcy said to her siblings. She and Melvin each took one of Jillisa's elbows and helped her hobble away.

"Be sure to let all your relatives know they'll have to look for work in the Kingston area," Mrs. Lynx called out, as if she were asking them to greet old friends. Kingston was the capital of the country, far on the eastern side. "It won't work out for them here anymore."

The kids didn't look back.

"You think dey will stay away?" Barney asked his boss.

Mrs. Lynx turned to Rupert. "We'll make sure they do, won't we, Rupert?"

Rupert nodded and hopped in his truck.

"Barney," said Mrs. Lynx, "I'm forced to come with you to the police station." She gave Lydia a tired look, as if Lydia had caused her to redo her homework, and then got in the passenger's seat of the 4Runner. "They're going to need a credible witness against Mr. Barnes."

Barney grinned. "That be right, ma'am," he said. "Come on," he said to the kids, not a hint of the schoolboy on his face—even though Lydia searched his eyes. "Get in de car."

They hadn't driven far when Lydia saw the Negril airport on their left—which was just the landing strip Lydia and her dad had flown into.

They passed by it, and Mrs. Lynx leaned forward in her seat. "Where are you going, Barney?"

"De police station, ma'am, just like you say."

"No, we have to get these kids to the airport first. Turn around."

"Okay, ma'am," Barney said, looking behind him to pull over. "I just be worried that woman she call get here before us."

Mrs. Lynx looked at her watch and sighed. "We've got an hour or so before their flight takes off. You're right. Keep going."

The two-story police station looked like the convenience store down the street from Lydia's old house in Indianapolis, except that it had bars on the windows over the glass. The building was tidy but small, and people hung around outside the doors. Lydia opened the car. Her dad was in there!

"Uh-uh, sweetie," Mrs. Lynx said. "You're staying here."

Barney jumped out and slammed Lydia's door shut again.

"But my dad's right there! I have to see him!"

"Sorry, darling," Mrs. Lynx said. "I'm afraid this would be too traumatic for you." She turned to Barney. "Keep an eye on them. I'll be back as soon as possible."

The moment Mrs. Lynx was out of sight, Lydia turned to Barney. "'Big Henry change he mind; I change mine too?'

What was that all about? I believed you! And you can change your—"

"Whoa, whoa, whoa," Barney said. His eyes were flitting back and forth as if he were thinking fast. "I know what I do."

"Yeah, right! You—"

"I take you to your dad," Barney said. "Come on, mon."

"That's more like it!" Lydia muttered as she jumped out of the car. Lydia walked quickly beside Barney as he strode to the station. Ben walked on the other side of him. "But are you going to change your mind again when Mrs. Lynx—"

"Shuddup, mon," Barney said. "I be thinking."

He opened the door and they all walked in.

Mrs. Lynx was sitting on a black plastic chair on the near side of a police officer's old metal desk. She looked up at the trio, concerned, but quickly changed her expression to one of great delight. Lydia knew better than to believe the woman's face reflected her true feelings.

"These are the children of Mr. Barnes, sir." Mrs. Lynx stood up and reached for Lydia's hand. "I've been looking out for them. I'm personally paying for their return trip to the United States, which departs later today. This whole situation simply breaks my h—"

"I got me something to say, Officer," Barney said. "And den you be putting me and dis here woman under arrest."

18
Missing Link

Mrs. Lynx actually jumped. She opened her mouth, but no words came out.

Lydia grabbed Barney's arm. "Don't, Barney! You'll go to jail!" she whispered.

The officer stood up and pulled up his huge pants by the waist. For a moment, the jingle of the keys on his hip was the only sound in the room. Mrs. Lynx started backing toward the door, but the officer nodded toward a guard, who immediately escorted Mrs. Lynx back to the black plastic chair and stood behind her.

"Go on," the officer said to Barney.

Barney shook Lydia off his arm and took a quick breath. "My name be Barney Bunk. I be working for Ms. Lynx these three years. She pay me to do many bad things."

Mrs. Lynx twitched.

"But de real trouble came dis week. Dis here lady had me start a fire at de schoolhouse near Cambellton two nights ago. And I stole a truck from dis girl's dad." He handed the officer the keys. "It be parked right outside. I kidnapped dis girl's schoolteacher and brought her to Mrs. Lynx. And when I caught de dad, Ms. Lynx gave me drugs to plant in de car and told me to accuse them of starting de fire. You got both these American here in you prison, and dey ain't done nothing wrong."

The officer moved toward him, and he held out his hands for the cuffs.

"Oh," Barney said as he held out his hands, "Ms. Lynx had me kidnap a couple other Jamaican kids. We was about to send these two back to America, and the other kids already been let go." He glanced at Mrs. Lynx. "I think."

Another nod from the officer, and the guard behind Mrs. Lynx was pulling out his cuffs. "You under arrest, ma'am, for—"

"It's all a lie!" Mrs. Lynx said, struggling to pull her hands away. "Those kids must be paying him to say these things. I'm innocent!"

"Nice try, Mrs. Lynx," the officer said. "But we know de whole story already. We had some outside help."

Lydia wasn't even listening to the officer. She turned to Barney. "What about your family?" she asked. The reason he worked for Mrs. Lynx in the first place, as he had told them back at Shark Bay, was to support them.

"Aw, . . ." Barney said, "I don' have no family."

"But you said—"

"Don't believe everything you hear, Miss Lydia," Barney said. "My parents dey left for Florida when I was jus' a boy, and dey quit sending barrels not much later. Since den I ain't even wanted to start my own family." He stopped in front of the doors and looked at Lydia. "I be glad to help a dad who look out for his kid. And other people's kids."

He nodded toward something behind her, and Lydia turned to see her dad and Mrs. Hinkle walking through a small doorway behind the officer's desk.

Lydia was crying before she got to him. "Daddy!"

Her father wrapped his smelly, dirty arms around her. "Pee-eww," she said between kisses as he covered the top of her head with all his love. "You stink."

"You can say that again," Mrs. Hinkle said. She was still wearing the same pajamas—full-length pink flannel boxers and a baggy pink T-shirt—she had been wearing the night of the fire, along with a little frown.

And then the door opened again.

Lydia and Ben looked at each other with their eyes and mouths wide open. Cynthia!

Ben got to her first. But Lydia didn't let that stop her. She rushed into the grandmotherly arms along with Ben. Lydia had forgotten how huge this woman's hug was, and how her wideness made her all the more beautiful. Cynthia Bell may never be an anorexic supermodel, but she would always be the most supermodel ever to Lydia. Cynthia had true beauty.

The officer caught Lydia's eye and smiled. "Yeah, your dad and de teacher had credible stories, but when Ms. Bell here flew in from Haiti an hour ago to say that you kids were missing, we be convinced. It just be a matter of figuring out de missing link." He looked at Barney. "That be you," he said.

"Me?"

"Yes. Your confession make de difference. You still be having to go to court to get a verdict, but we have enough evidence now to let these Americans go."

The guards began to lead Mrs. Lynx and Barney toward the doorway the others had just come from, but Lydia ran to Barney and hugged him. "Don't worry, Barney. We'll send you barrels and barrels of food and books and blankets and stuff. We won't forget about you."

"Tank you, Lydia," Barney said. "But I ain't worried. I feel better now than I be feeling in years." His toothless grin was gorgeous.

Mrs. Lynx didn't look like she was feeling better, though. She was arguing with the guards and trying to break free as they led her through the door. Barney followed behind, whistling.

Lydia ran back to her father's hug. She was dirty and hungry with no possessions except the clothes on her back, but she felt happier than she ever had at the ritziest resort on the island.

But things were not perfect yet. "We have to hurry, Dad!" Lydia said. "Jillisa and Melvin are walking all the way back to the village. And Rupert might be after them!"

19
Secret of Shark Bay

The police officer gave Frank the keys to the 4Runner, and the GRO crew dashed out the door. Hink went in Cynthia's car and Lydia climbed in the passenger seat next to her dad in the 4Runner. Ben sat behind Lydia.

Frank led the way up the main street of Negril with the ocean waving to them from the left. Normally he got at least one speeding ticket a year, but now he was barely crawling down the street.

"Dad! Quit driving so slow!"

"Hitting tourists would not make this trip go any faster," he said.

Lydia watched the little shops and restaurants that lined the streets and actually wished that these places she would normally love to wander through would disappear. It was weird to think that just a few days ago she had been hoping for a week on the beach herself. Now what she wanted most in the world was to go out into the jungle and teach kids to read.

"How long will it take for us to rebuild the schoolhouse?" she asked her dad.

"Oh, with the right crew and equipment, it should take less than a week. As soon as we get home, I'll hire a contractor and enlist some volunteers to get out there."

"Can't we just do it ourselves?"

"No, Peachoo. We're going home tomorrow."

"Tomorrow?"

"Yes, as planned. Which is good, because we need to get some education into you. These trips are seriously interfering with that."

Lydia disagreed. She was learning more than she ever had back home.

Lydia's phone rang. It was Cynthia. "Sweetheart," the woman said when Lydia picked up. "I heard you make the lovely promise to Mr. Bunk that you would send him food. I'm not sure that task is feasible for Global Relief to take on—"

"But he'll die without help!" Lydia said. "They don't provide food for the prisoners, and he doesn't have any fam—"

"Lydia," Frank whispered. "Don't interrupt." He must have been able to hear Cynthia's voice carrying through the cell.

"Exactly," Cynthia said. "He'll be sent to Kingston, and he'll be terribly neglected at the prison there. That's why I just made some phone calls. A ministry in Kingston will bring food to him every day."

"Oh." Lydia blushed. She really had to learn to keep her mouth shut. "What ministry is it?"

"An organization that is similar to ours in Cambellton. Only this school specializes in teaching adults to read by using Bible stories. And they have volunteers who go into the prison to teach any who are interested in learning how to read. I'm not sure whether he'll bite or not, but lessons will at least be offered to him."

Lydia laughed. God sure knew how to work things out. And using Cynthia was a pretty good way for him to get it done. Now she just hoped he would use her painfully slow-driving dad to save her friends.

They passed out of Negril and drove five miles on the road the kids would have walked to get back home.

"Keep going, Dad," Lydia insisted. "They've got to be here."

"They couldn't have walked farther than this," Frank said. "Not with Jillisa's ankle so bad."

Ben stuck his face between the seats with his arms on the backs of the seats. "Maybe they got off the road when they saw the 4Runner because they thought it was Barney."

Or maybe Rupert got them off the road for another reason altogether.

"Let's go back to the Luxury Resort," Frank said. "Maybe we'll find this Rupert guy."

Lydia nodded. There didn't seem to be anything else to do.

Rupert was nowhere to be seen at the Luxury Resort, but the British man, Tom Adams, was.

"Frank Barnes?" he called out. "What's going on, old chap? I've been hearing terrible rumors about you."

Lydia sat cross-legged on the beach, restless, listening to her dad tell Tom and all the others who had gathered around that Mrs. Lynx had the story all wrong. And everyone had questions.

"Yes," Frank said, "Lydia really was attacked by a shark. Apparently Mrs. Lynx was dumping excess food into the water a few miles down, and it was attracting sharks. I've already called the Marine Police about it, and they're dealing with the problem.

"Yes," he said, "I was in jail, but only because Mrs. Lynx framed me for her own crimes.

"Yes," he said, "the school was burned down and we're in desperate need of assistance. Any of you who want to donate time, money, or books may certainly do so."

"Lydia," Ben said suddenly, tugging on her arm. "Look!"

Lydia turned around and saw Melvin, Jillisa, and Marcy walking in the front door of the Luxury Resort.

The twins looked around anxiously and Marcy looked determined, but when they saw that the blurs coming straight for them were Lydia and Ben, they all screamed with delight. "What are you doing here? How did you escape?"

"Mrs. Lynx is in jail!" Ben said.

"My dad and Mrs. Hinkle are free!" Lydia said. "But what about you? We were looking for you! What are you doing here?"

Before they could answer, Frank walked over and introduced himself to Marcy.

"I been hearing wonderful things 'bout you, Mister Barnes," she said.

"Call me Frank."

Marcy smiled. "Thank you for all you been doing for my brother and sister—and for my village. But, please, does Ms. Lynx be in jail for real?"

"Yes," Frank said, "and I expect she'll be there for quite some time. Barney is there too. We can tell you all about it on the drive back home."

Marcy's eyebrows scrunched down and she put her pointer fingers up by her chin.

"What are you thinking about?" Lydia asked.

"I—" Marcy pulled her hands down and looked up at Frank. "I don't think I be going back to de village. I be staying here to run de resort." When she saw Frank's confused expression she said, "I be de assistant manager here. I be de only one who can run dis here place now."

"You can't be staying, Marcy!" Jillisa said. "I want you back with us. And you be fired, remember?"

Marcy smiled at her. "No one but Barney and Rupert know 'bout that."

"But Marcy—"

"You don' need to worry, Jilly. I be visiting more. But dey need me here."

"Who need you?"

"All de people I work with, de guests, even Ms. Lynx."

"What bout Shark Bay?" Melvin asked.

"Soon," Marcy said. She smiled.

"Am I missing something?" Lydia asked.

"Come," Marcy said, lifting her head and looking suddenly professional, "you sit here. We have much to talk about." She led them to a quiet table at the edge of the patio overlooking the ocean. "Please wait here." She went to the front desk and began chatting with the lady there.

"What's going on?" Mrs. Hinkle asked.

"Marcy tell you," Melvin said. But he giggled.

The gang sat quietly, watching Marcy direct another employee of the resort. A few minutes later she came back.

"Would you like anything to eat or drink?" she asked, standing next to them.

"Just sit down, Marcy," Melvin said. "They be wanting to know about Shark Bay."

Marcy smiled and sat down. She crossed her legs and smiled again. "Rupert, he be my cousin's husband."

"The cousin you live with?" Frank asked.

"Yessah," Marcy said. "I be staying at their house when I not be working at de resort. And my cousin, she be worried 'bout Rupert. He never be home. He be hanging with de wrong people. But my cousin, she know that Rupert be a good man at heart."

Frank nodded. "If he's anything like Barney, I have no doubt."

Marcy smiled again. "When Rupert found out his job be to kidnap me, and that his other prisoners be my kid brother and sister, he got scared. He told his wife he wanted out of the business, but he don' know how to quit. He don't think he had a choice."

"There is always a choice," Lydia said. She thought of all the choices she could have made over the last few days and how differently things would have turned out.

Marcy nodded. "Yeah, that be why as soon as Barney and Ms. Lynx left with you"—she looked at Ben and Lydia—"Rupert came after us and took us to his place."

"So why did you come back here?"

Marcy laughed. "Rupert had a plan. He was mad that Ms. Lynx had called Shark Bay her land," Marcy said. "Remember, when she ran us off?"

Ben and Lydia nodded. "What's so bad about that?"

"Shark Bay, that be his land," Marcy said. "It been in de family all these years. Rupert told Ms. Lynx 'bout it once to show off, and she took it over. She took the deed and locked it up in her safe. She say to help him, but he know better."

"It's his land?" Frank murmured. "That's amazing."

"Yeah!" Marcy said. "I tell him we be opening a resort there. I be his manager. His wife, she can read. She be real smart, and she can manage de books." Marcy smiled, clearly prouder of herself than if she had put that shark in a headlock and knocked its teeth out.

Lydia took a deep breath. Shark Bay was gorgeous, but there was one little problem. Sharks. "Um, your guests might not like swimming there."

Frank put his palm on the table. "I can help with that."

"Dad, don't let this hero thing get to your head. You can't knock out every shark in the ocean."

Frank laughed. "No, I wouldn't want to. But I've been told that the Marine Police intend to install some sort of mesh fence to block the sharks from entering the bay. It should take just a few months until they get bored and go back to their regular feeding pattern."

"But, Marcy, you be wanting to run a resort?" Jillisa asked. "I don't want you to be like Ms. Lynx."

Marcy nodded. "Yeah, I want to run de resort, Jilly. This be a great opportunity for me, plus I would pay decent wages to my people. Ms. Lynx, she be a bad woman; but she be a good hotel manager. I be learning so much from her. And Shark Bay, it gonna be beautiful." She looked up, and Lydia could almost see the mental image Marcy must have been looking at. "Dis resort, it gonna show de true nature of this country. Guests gonna rest and play, yeah. But dey gonna learn 'bout Jamaica too. I be praying that their hearts be filling with a love for dis country and for Jamaicans so next time dey come, dey be coming to serve."

Frank looked at her as if she were the most gorgeous sunset over the Caribbean Sea.

But Ben didn't look so thrilled. "Do you really think you'll get any guests with a name like Shark Bay Resort?"

Marcy laughed. "We going to change the name. We can choose whatever name we like."

"I want to work for you, Marcy," Melvin said.

"Me too," Jillisa added.

"Me too," Lydia said.

"Uh-uh," Mrs. Hinkle said, and everyone looked at her, surprised. "You kids all need to finish your schooling first. Then you can go on to choose whatever job you like."

Jillisa looked at Marcy, who nodded. "She be right. You go to school first."

"Talking about choosing whatever we like," Frank said, "do you think the manager of this little place would let us enjoy the buffet? I'm hungry."

Marcy laughed and stood up. "Oh, yessah! Please stay de night here. There be work to do."

"Work?" Ben asked.

"Yeah, mon! I started getting books and stuff like you kids were doing. Ms. Lynx, she found out and fired me, but now can't stop us."

Lydia jumped up. "Let's do it!"

"Uh, not so fast, missy," Mrs. Hinkle said. "Tomorrow will be soon enough. Today you have school."

Perhaps it was Jillisa's squeal of delight, or Lydia's own attempt at teaching that morning, or Mrs. Hinkle's heroic act on behalf of Melvin—Lydia didn't know what prompted her to do such a crazy thing. But suddenly she was hugging her miserable teacher in front of the whole world without caring who saw her. "You're not so bad, Mrs. Hinkle," Lydia said.

"That's Hink, if you please." And for the first time since Lydia had known her, Hink actually shot her a big smile.